THE SONG OF THE TIDES

The Song of Octa
A novella

JAMES CALBRAITH

FLYING
SQUID

Published December 2021 by Flying Squid

Visit James Calbraith's official website at
jamescalbraith.wordpress.com
for the latest news, book details, and other information

Copyright © James Calbraith, 2021

This book is a work of fiction. Names, characters, places and incidents either are products of the author's imagination or are used fictitiously. Any resemblance to actual events or locales or persons, living or dead, is entirely coincidental.

All rights reserved. Except as permitted under the U.S. Copyright Act of 1976, no part of this publication may be reproduced, distributed or transmitted in any form or by any means, or stored in a database or retrieval system, without the prior written permission of the publisher.
Fan fiction and fan art is encouraged.

ARMORICA, C. 460 AD

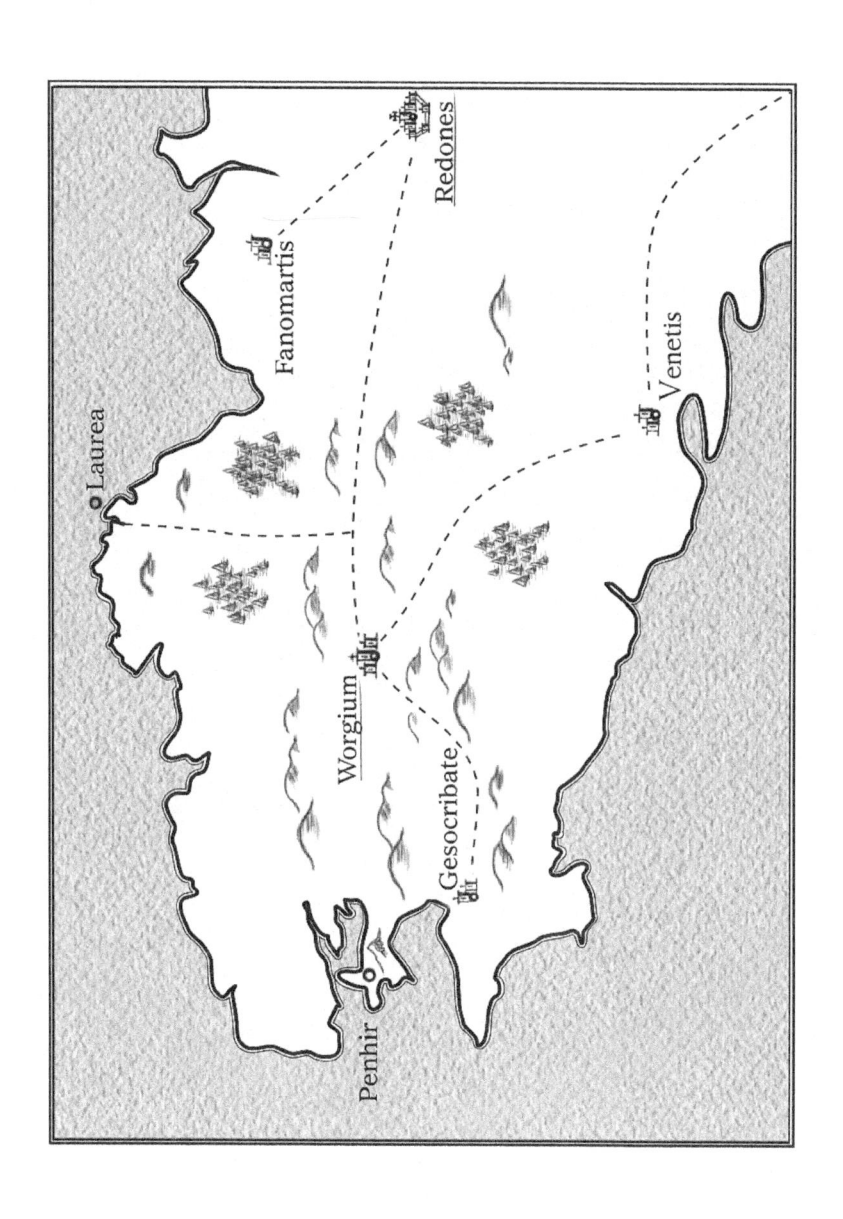

CAST OF CHARACTERS

Britannia

Aelle: *Rex* of the Saxons
Aeric I: *Rex* of the Iutes
Ambrosius: *Dux* of Britannia Prima
Betula: *Gesith*, commander of King Aeric's household guards
Fastidius: Bishop of Londin, brother of King Aeric
Honorius: Ambrosius's son
Madron: daughter of Wortimer, former *Dux* of Britannia Maxima, and Rhedwyn
Riotham: Councillor of Londin, Ambrosius's representative

Octa: *aetheling* of Iutes, son of King Aeric
Ursula: daughter of Cantian nobles, Octa's bride

Octa's riders:
    Audulf
    Croha
    Deor
    Eolh
    Haering
    Hleo
    Picga
    Seawine
    Ubba

Armorica

Cado: surgeon in Marcus's detachment
Drustan: young officer in Marcus's detachment
Marcus: *Decurion* of a cavalry detachment from Dumnonia
Mullo: former Legionnaire

Rhion: leader of the Bacaud rebels
Wenelia: Rhion's wife, leader of the Bacaud rebels

Ahes: daughter of Graelon, *Comes* of Armorican Britons
Budic: Armorican Briton patrician
Graelon: *Comes* of Armorican Britons
Maegwind: Graelon's wife
Warus: Captain of *Maegwind*, Graelon's flagship
Constantin: Priest from Worgium

Aegidius: *Magister Militum* of Gaul
Hildrik: king of the Salian Franks

Goths

Eishild: daughter of Thaurismod, rightful king of the Goths
Fridurik: brother of Theodrik, king of the Goths
Hemnerith: brother of Theodrik, king of the Goths
Theodrik: king of the Goths

GLOSSARY

Aetheling: member of the Iutish royal family
Angon: barbed throwing spear
Centuria: troop of (about) hundred infantry
Centurion: officer in Roman infantry
Chrismon: a monogram symbol of Christ
Comes, pl. Comites: administrator of a *pagus*, subordinate to the *Dux*
Decurion: officer in Roman cavalry
Domus: the main structure of a *villa*
Domnus, Domna: Roman lord and lady
Dux: overall commander in war times; in peace time — administrator of a province
Equites: Roman cavalry
Francisca: throwing axe
Frauja, fraujo: Lord and lady in Frankish
Fyrd: army made up of all warriors of the tribe
Gardingi: household guard of the Gothic king
Gesith: companion of the *Drihten*, chief of the *Hiréd*
Hiréd: band of elite warriors of *Drihten*'s household
Hlaford, Hlaefdige: Lord and Lady in Saxon tongue.
Liburna: Roman warship
Mansio: staging post
Pagus, pl. Pagi: administrative unit, smaller than a province
Plumbata: Roman throwing dart
Rex: king of a barbarian tribe
Rix: king of the Goths
Seax: Saxon short sword
Spatha: Roman long sword
Torc: a metal neck ring
Villa: Roman agricultural property
Vigiles: town guards and firemen
Wealh, pl. wealas: "the others", Britons in Saxon tongue.

PLACE NAMES

Andreda: Weald Forest
Ariminum: Wallington, Surrey
Armorica: Brittany
Aurelianum: Orleans, France
Cair Inis: Ile Tristan, Brittany
Cantia: Kent
Dorowern: Dorovernum, Canterbury, Kent
Dubris: Dover, France
Dumnonia: Cornwall and Devon
Dumnonian Isca: Isca Dumnoniorum, Exeter, Cornwall
Gesocribate: Douarnenez, Brittany
Laurea: Ile-de-Brehat, Brittany
Liger: River Loire
Lenur: Jersey Island
New Port: Novus Portus, Portslade, Sussex
Redones: Rennes, Brittany
Rhenum: River Rhine
Robriwis: Dorobrivis, Rochester, Kent
Rotomag: Rotomagus, Rouen, France
Rutubi: Rutupiae, Richborough, Kent
Tolosa: Toulouse, France
Trever: Trier, France
Worgium: Carhaix, Brittany

CANTIA, 461 AD

CHAPTER I
THE LAY OF HONORIUS

A dozen pony riders charge in a tight wedge from the Roman road, flanked by a few light footmen on either side. They ride up the spur of the hill, the ponies struggling in the sand and mud. Up on the hill, just outside the circle of wooden stakes, stand the spearmen; not in a straight wall, but a diagonal line, with Seawine and three of his best men holding the left flank, and the rest of his warriors set up behind and to his right.

Just before the riders strike, Seawine cries an order. His warriors stamp their oblong shields into the ground and push forth their spears, topped with wooden training blades. The cavalry wedge smashes into the line; the spears shatter, the shields break. The footmen on the sides engage Seawine's flanks but are soon repelled by the heavy axemen he kept in reserve. His own side holds, but further down the riders' wedge unravels along the line in a series of individual duels: horse against spear, lance against shield. The fight doesn't last long. The shield wall wobbles, then breaks in the centre. At Seawine's command, the surviving shieldsmen turn in an effort to trap the riders that got through, but they're too late. The first of the ponies reaches the palisade. Its rider leaps from the saddle, climbs over the stakes to the wooden tower behind and, with a triumphant roar, raises the banner of the white dragon over the rampart.

I descend from my raised watch point and applaud her for the victory. Ursula bows mockingly. Seawine and the others pick themselves up from the ground, rub their bruises and join in the cheers.

The Song of the Tides

I come up to the wall and help Ursula down, then turn to Seawine.

"Not bad," I tell him, "but against the Boar Snout you should've used Wolf's Jaws, not a Snake's Bite."

"I know, *aetheling*," Seawine replies with a grin. "I wanted to try something else this time."

"I value your resourcefulness, *Gesith*. Who knows, there may be a time when a Snake's Bite is the correct response."

"But this wasn't it," says Ursula. She punches Seawine on the shoulder.

"What was that for?" he asks.

"Your spear." She throws off the Frankish bearskin that she and Seawine wear as a mark of seniority, lifts her tunic and shows a swiftly darkening bruise on her side.

"You cheated!" Seawine laughs. "You'd never get on that rampart with a wound like that!"

Ursula scoffs. "Maybe I'd bleed out afterwards, but I wouldn't let a scratch like this keep me from an easy victory."

A booming laughter, coming from the foot of the hill, interrupts our bickering. I look down to see my father, Aeric, king of the Iutes, on the back of his faithful mount, Frige, staring at us with amusement.

"*Hlaford!*" Seawine exclaims. The younger warriors kneel down before him and lower their heads. Only Ursula and I remain standing – myself, because I'm his son and prospective heir, should the *Witan* so decide after his death; Ursula, because she's not his subject. She's a *wealh*, a free Briton, fighting on our side out of choice and friendship, rather than duty.

I run-and-slide down the muddy slope to greet him. His guard is some distance away, on the outskirts of an abandoned *villa* we chose as the site of our exercise. It's some three miles from one of my father's mead halls in the ancient fortress of Rutubi, on the old highway to the Dubris harbour. It's near enough for us to retire after the battles, and yet far enough to allow us to stay out of sight and out of the way of the *real Hiréd*, my father's household guard, stationed at Rutubi.

Unless, for some reason, they all decide to come here to witness our efforts.

"Interesting. You are more like your uncle Fastid than myself," my father notes. "But then, he did spend more time with you when you were a child…"

"How do you mean?"

"Back at Ariminum, it was Fastid who would come up with the strategies, and watch from a distance, while your mother and I would work to put them into practice – just like Ursula and Seawine. What do you call this pattern?"

"A Snake's Bite."

"Vegetius calls it a Ladder."

"I know, Father. That's where I got it from. The Battle of Leuctra."

The Song of the Tides

I learn all my stratagems from my studies of the old Roman books, a trove of which was given to me three years ago in Trever by Rav Asher – as a reward for our help in saving the city from the Saxon siege. There is more knowledge of war in those books than I could ever learn from observing the king's *Hiréd*, who are the finest warriors in the tribe. Not just descriptions of ancient battles, the tactics and strategies used in the conflicts as great and famous as Hannibal's War or Alexander's conquests – but manuals for laying and defending from sieges, plans of war engines, even instructions on such minutiae as gathering necessary provisions for the campaign, or how often a Legion should break camp, depending on how fast it's going...

Most of this knowledge is useless here, on the edge of Britannia, a generation after Rome abandoned the island to barbarians like ourselves. The Legions are gone and, with them, gone is the age of great battles that engaged thousands of men on each side. A Iute warband doesn't need to break camp to march to war – Cantia is small enough to cross it in a day. My father owns a single siege engine, guarding the Medu at Robriwis, and it is enough to hold back any enemy foolish enough to attempt crossing that river.

All that remains for me, then, is to study the disposition of troops, and the simple formations into which I can arrange my men. I gave these Roman patterns names that my Iutes would find easier to grasp – Snake's Bite for the Ladder Line, Wolf Jaws for the Inverted Cuneus, and so on. Only the Boar Snout isn't one of my own – the Iutes and Saxons have been using it since before crossing the whale road, back in the Old Country, and all of my father's warriors are trained in using it to break the enemy shield walls.

"What brings you here, Father?" I ask. "I didn't know you were coming to watch us."

"And I didn't plan to," he replies. "I came to bring you news. We have a visitor from the West at Rutubi. Someone I thought you'd be pleased to see."

"And you couldn't have sent a messenger to tell us that?" I ask, frowning.

"And miss a chance to see my son recreate the scenes from my youth?"

He grins and pats me on the head. I know what he means. When he was a few years younger than myself and lived as a slave foundling on the grounds of a Briton nobleman's *villa*, he would exercise in just the same manner as us, with his friends and other youths from the nearby villages. One of those friends was now the Bishop of Londin himself, His Grace Fastidius. The other was my poor mother, Eadgith, the bladesmith's daughter…

"You were merely playing back then," I tell him. "We are training for war. My *Hiréd* are just as good as yours."

My father nods. "I don't doubt that. Your friend Colswine is now part of my personal retinue." He nods towards the guards in the village. "And you know Betula's not letting just anyone under her command."

He sits back up and tugs gently on the reins. Frige turns in place.

"But you're right, Octa. I could've sent a messenger. I am, in fact, on my way to Dubris. We have more visitors coming, and these ones I want to greet myself."

"More visitors?" I scratch my head. I can't remember what day it is – I barely remember the month. Days all blur together here in Cantia; we've had an uneventful peace for the past three years, protected by our alliances with the Franks and Gauls on one side, and the Britons on the other. Even Aelle's Saxons have been keeping quiet, not daring to strike at a king who is friend to Hildrik, *Rex* of the powerful Salians.

"Is it time already?" I ask, finally remembering.

"Not quite yet," my father replies. "But it's soon enough."

Three horses – large war horses of the Britons, rather than our small ponies – stand tied before the entrance to the guesthouse, built just outside the walls of Rutubi to accommodate the visitors to the king's *burh*, his fortified dwelling. Just as I'm about to enter to see who the new guests are, one of them emerges from the outhouse.

"Mullo!" I cry and rush to greet him. We slap each other on the backs; his slam beats the breath out of my lungs.

"What are you doing here?" I ask.

We sit on the grass outside the guesthouse. This isn't a tavern – there's no kitchen here, and only a common room around the central hearth in place of the dining hall: too small to fit us all. Rutubi isn't a Briton town, after all, just a small settlement raised around my father's court for his guards and servants. When *Rex* Aeric moves to Robriwis or Leman, life here all but ceases for the rest of the year.

I stop a passing serf and tell her to bring us mead and ale. She bows and runs to fetch the drink from the alewife's hut.

"I'm in *Dux* Ambrosius's forward guard," Mullo explains. "We're in Londin, to make sure everything's ready for his arrival."

"Did anyone else come with you?" asks Seawine.

"It's just me. All of Marcus's men went back with him to Dumnonia – he's the *Praetor* at Dun Taiel now. And the Atecots are still not as welcome in Corin as they deserve…"

The serf girl brings us two heavy jugs, brimming with ale and mead. Mullo takes a long gulp, ending with a satisfying belch.

"You heathens know how to brew," he says. "I've missed this. The Britons are always trying too hard. Ambrosius insists on serving wine at his capital, but it's sour like vinegar."

"I'm surprised you haven't returned to Gaul," says Seawine. "If you're missing good drink this much."

"Gaul has become too peaceful under Aegidius," Mullo replies with a wince. "For a mercenary seeking good pay and easy fighting, there were only two choices – Armorica or Britannia, and I didn't fancy serving under the likes of Graelon or Budic."

The Song of the Tides

He looks around. "Where's Ursula?" he asks. "Your father told me she's training with you."

"She's gone to Dorowern to prepare. We'll pick her up on our way to Londin."

"She doesn't live with you? Don't tell me you two still haven't properly wedded…"

"She says there's no need, yet, as long as we're both safe in Cantia." I shrug. "And I don't want to press her."

Ursula and I were wedded, in a pagan ceremony, three years ago, in Frankia – our hands fastened before the gods by Meroweg, king of the Salians. But the ritual was false, a ruse which enabled Meroweg's son, Hildrik, to slay his father and take over the kingdom. Ever since then, our relationship could at best be described as "complicated".

"Well, if you're not wedded to her in the eyes of law and God, that leaves you free to other pursuits," Mullo remarks. "Lord knows I wouldn't pass the opportunity." He glances towards the shieldmaiden chucking flying axes at a target attached to the fort's crumbling wall. "I heard tales of the beauty of the Iutish women, but they all fall short of reality."

"Croha – a beauty?" I laugh incredulously.

The girl throwing the axes is Croha; my father found her orphaned on Wecta and brought her back some seven years ago. She's now all grown up, and one of the young warriors training to gain entry into the ranks of my father's *Hiréd* guards.

"Does love for Ursula blind you so much?" asks Mullo.

"I've known this one since she was a little girl," I say. "She's more like a sister to me."

I take another glance at Croha, trying to look at her with the eyes of another man, and to my surprise, I have to admit Mullo is right. Croha's once-mousy hair has turned into a river of gold, and her maiden body has grown into that of a fine, muscle-bound woman, even if the mail shirt and the cloak thrown over it conceal some of her best features.

She notices my gaze and stands to attention, to present herself as a dutiful guard before her *aetheling*. I turn back to Mullo, feeling my cheeks turn red.

"When does the *Dux* arrive?" I ask.

"In three days," he replies, then leans closer and lowers his voice. "It's yet a secret, but I can tell you already – this will not be as grand a ceremony as would befit the occasion. We were only told to secure rooms in a single inn."

"How come?"

Mullo scowls. "Things aren't going great for Ambrosius. The treasury is as empty as a Saxon whore's bed at Pascha. The Picts ravaged the Demet coast, and the less said about the Brigants, the better… Even the Belgs are growing restless again, preferring to side with their Saxon kin than be ruled from Corin. The only direction we're *not* being attacked from is Hibernia – and that's only because Cunedag is doing such a good job protecting our frontier. Some at the court are saying he should be the *Dux* instead."

"Then there's peace between Cunedag and the Britons? Just as Wortigern had hoped?"

He shrugs. "A peace born of necessity. We have no force with which to fight him, even if we wanted to. His men took all the forts up to Teibi, and nobody bothered to stop them. And as long as he keeps the Scots away from the *villas* and the towns – who would complain?"

"I always said there was nothing worth fighting for in Wened," I say. "Still," I add, "you'd think the *Dux* wouldn't spare gold on his only son's betrothal to the last surviving heir of Wortigern."

"Oh, he will throw a great feast back in Corin, when it's all done. But why spend gold here – to impress a few Londin noblemen and a handful of barbarians?" Mullo shakes his head. "At least, that's what I think is happening. I'm not a courtier. I'm just a mercenary in the court's employ. I only repeat what the others are saying. You'll see for yourself soon."

He looks into the mead jug. "There's more than half left," he says. "Do you think I can ask that beautiful shieldmaiden to join me in finishing it off?"

"It won't hurt to try," I reply with an uneasy grin.

The vaulted, incense-filled hall of Londin's Saint Paul's is the greatest chamber in all of Britannia still in use – at least, so the city folk like to tell themselves – and the only one large enough to accommodate the crowd that fills it today. It rises like a mountain of black and white marble, on top of a hill in the south-eastern corner of the city, three hundred feet long and half as wide, a looming symbol of the only power still able to control the resources of the island to raise such a monument: the Church.

But the ceremony for which we have gathered is not a rite of the Church. Bishop Fastidius would not conduct the betrothal. "My word, I fear, would fasten the children as firmly as the word of God himself," he told us. "Neither the princess, nor the *Dux*'s boy would be able to unravel these binds." He is here, nonetheless, to the right of the altar, surrounded by his acolytes and observing the proceedings carefully. In his place – not at the altar itself, for that space is sacred, but just in front of it – is Riotham, the nobleman who represents *Dux* Ambrosius's interests at the Londin Council.

Most of the people in the crowd in the cathedral and outside it are regular city folk, arriving out of boredom and curiosity to see what these days is a rare occasion in Londin's subdued, quiet life: a gathering of all the nobles of the province, come to witness the betrothal. There are strangers among them, too: merchants from the harbour district; representatives of neighbouring heathen tribes – though not of Aelle and his Saxons; envoys from Britannia's other provincial capitals, Ebrauc and Lindocoln. The most important of the guests, however, the most exotic, and commanding the greatest interest of the congregation, is the delegation of Salian Franks, led by their *Rex* himself, Hildrik.

It was to greet him that my father went to Dubris. Hildrik arrived on the same old *liburna* that once brought legate Aegidius to our shores, in the full regalia of a Roman Imperial officer, except for the bear fur cape thrown over the red tunic embroidered with the golden eagle, and the circlet of a Frankish king upon his brow. Coming on the same ship was Audulf, sent with a small band of warriors to fight the slave raiders in Frisia; they brought back another handful of freed Iutes and a chest of plunder.

"You are a *legatus* now, *Rex* Hildrik?" I asked, after we exchanged warm greetings at Rutubi mead hall. It had been three years since we last saw each other, though we managed to keep in touch through missives and messengers. This, however, was news to me.

"More than that, Octa. I am the *Comes* of Toxandria and a *Magister* in command of the Frankish auxiliaries."

"But you're still the king of the Salians?"

"Indeed. I rule my people without Rome's interference, and Aegidius pays us to protect his borders."

"A fine agreement," I said, thinking of Ambrosius's troubles with Cunedag – and about my father. The Britons had no gold to pay us for the protection they enjoyed behind the backs of our warriors – or rather, as my father suspected, didn't wish to part with it even when threatened by raiders and pirates. So they gave us land, instead. Hildrik, it seemed, received both as reward for his services. "And you did well from it," I added, noting the gilded, jewel-studded hilt of his sword and thick bands of sculpted gold on his shoulders.

"If it can last," Hildrik replied with a sudden frown.

"Trouble?"

Hildrik and his messengers have been my main – though not the only – source of news from the Continent for these past few years. Eager to assist my father in this new diplomacy, I try my best to keep up with what goes on in

Gaul and beyond, so that at least my mind can travel to these distant places even if I myself am stuck here in Britannia.

"Maybe it's nothing." He shrugged. "Rumours from Rome, again. Some say the Imperator's dead. And if he is, that might mean another war…" He cheered up again. "But, let's not talk about such matters before such an auspicious day. I brought the skins you asked for." He waved at his men, each carrying a heavy bundle of bearskin coats. "Two dozen, just as you requested. My hunters went as far as the River Albi to get them."

"I am most grateful."

"It's the least I could do for the man who brought me my kingdom!" he said, beaming, and slapped me on the back.

Now, in the cathedral, he stands a few feet away from me, surrounded by his armed retinue. They're the only ones allowed to bear arms in the cathedral – not even the bishop dared to challenge a band of Frankish warriors, allies to the Empire. Hildrik notices me and nods; I nod back. Just then, the trumpets announce the arrival of the betrothed couple.

This is the first time I see Honorius, Ambrosius's son. The *Dux* waited a long time for an heir – he's not much younger than his once-counterpart in the East, Wortigern, and yet his son is only twelve years old. He looks like any other Briton child, dark haired and dark eyed, with pouty lips and rosy cheeks. Dressed in robes of gold and purple, gleaming in the light of candles and oil lamps, he approaches the altar led by his father. Ambrosius hasn't been seen in the city since Wortimer's War, nine years ago, and there are many here who still scowl at his presence, if silently: he is a guest of the bishop, of the Council – and of the Iutes. My people may

The Song of the Tides

only be allowed to settle east of the Medu River, a day's march from Londin's walls, but they command as much fear and respect in the city as if we held its gates. Our friendship with the Franks makes us friends of Rome itself; I myself had more contact with Roman officials during my adventures in Gaul than many of Londin's nobles. Our fortresses on the Tamesa guard the merchant routes that keep the city fed and diverted. Our fields provide produce for its markets.

And now, my father is about to become even more powerful. He is already the guardian to little *Domna* Madron, replacing in this task her grandfather, *Dux* Wortigern; through her betrothal with Honorius, he will become kin to Ambrosius — and few in Londin can make such a claim.

Ambrosius steps forward now, pushing the girl gently to stand beside Honorius. I still think of her sometimes as Myrtle, daughter of Princess Rhedwyn, the shy little Iutish girl I first saw in Cunedag's hillfort, in the windswept moors of Wened; I did not yet know then that she is my kin, too, for her mother was, secretly, my father's sister. The girl has spent the past three years under the tutelage of Bishop Fastidius — as I had, once — and though still very young, she presents herself more like a Briton princess than a barbarian maiden. Dressed all in white, with a veil rolled over her hair, she bows, gracefully, first before Riotham, and next her soon-to-be betrothed and then turns to bow before the entire congregation.

Riotham recites a short preamble, invoking God's grace — though he's careful not to depend on the Lord's will too much, keenly aware of the bishop's piercing gaze. The swift and concise manner in which he speaks tells me Mullo was right: this is going to be a brief ceremony, after all.

[24]

"Let us now hear the oaths of *Domnus* Honorius, son of Ambrosius," Riotham declares into the echoing silence, "and *Domna* Madron, daughter of Wortimer."

A murmur spreads throughout the rear of the cathedral, and outside, into the crowd gathered in the light of day. Not all, it seems, of those gathered were aware of what's taking place today; neither Madron's lineage, nor her presence in the capital were common knowledge – she has rarely stepped outside the cathedral walls. I wonder what the regular city folk think of what is happening. A daughter of Wortimer, the last *Dux* in Londin, the bloody tyrant – were they even aware she existed?

Honorius reaches out to Riotham and hands him three golden coins. "With these three coins," he says, in pure Imperial Latin – his voice is thin, wobbly, distorted by the echoes dancing under the great vault – "I buy the promise of your hand, Madron."

"I consent to this promise," Madron replies. She speaks clearly and boldly, with her head held high. She is the first to reach for the parchment Riotham presents the two, and to sign her name under the document. When Honorius then struggles with putting the iron ring on her third finger, she takes it from him impatiently and puts it on herself.

Ursula, standing to my right, observes the girl with eyes gleaming with pride, as if it was her own daughter taking part in the ceremony. In the years of Madron's stay in the cathedral, no man was allowed to see her other than the bishop and his acolytes; instead, it was Ursula, in my father's name, and a certain slave called Antonia, in Riotham's employ, who were checking in on the girl's well-being. As a result, Ursula's fondness for Madron has grown even stronger than it already was when we first met the girl in the cold, distant hills of Wened.

Riotham joins their hands together. "*Nubo,*" says Madron, "I am veiled." She drops the veil over her face; a symbol that, from now until wedlock, her eyes and lips belong to no one but her betrothed.

This is an old Roman ritual, still heathen in its rustic simplicity. I imagine one like it being performed countless times in the ancient temples that once stood in the city's centre, before Christian priests banished the old gods all into the hills and forests. Other than Riotham's invocation, there is no mention of the Lord on the parchment, only a dry list of dowries and gifts to be exchanged between the two families.

"It is done," Riotham announces and raises the signed document into the light. Ambrosius and my father step forward to inspect it, then salute each other with their fists to their chests — and take the children away as the crowd behind us erupts in cheers.

Mullo's predictions came true — two days after the betrothal, having finished all his discussions with the Council and audiences with the Briton nobles, Ambrosius and his courtiers pack their trunks and set off back towards Corin without much ceremony. Just before his procession passes through the Callew Gate, I receive word that the *Dux* wishes to speak to me in person.

"Ah, young Octa," the *Dux* calls, bidding me to come closer to his lectern.

[26]

"Lord *Dux*." I salute and bow. "You seem to be in a great hurry to go back. Do you not like it here in Londin?"

"Oh, I like the city – love it, in fact. My father's old capital, after all… It's the people I'm not partial to. All the decent Londin folk left after Wortimer's death." He sighs. "Two days was more than enough. Every noble from New Port to Lindocoln wanted to have an audience with me. I had to run away, or they'd have bored me to death. And every one of them wanting gifts and favours!" He rolls his eyes. "It's *they* that should be giving gifts to *me*!"

"You did not partake in any of Londin's pleasures then, lord *Dux?* Theatre, baths?"

He waves his hand. "We have those in Corin. Better than here. In truth, being here only brings melancholy. It reminds me of how great a city it really was in the days of my youth. It's like looking at your beloved, perishing from disease of old age." He smiles, sadly. "Still, who knows what the future will bring? It might regain its old glories one day – though not in my lifetime, and I doubt if even in yours, young Octa." He pats my hand. "It's a pity we haven't had a chance to talk while I was in the city."

"I didn't think you'd be keen to see me, considering what happened the last time we saw each other."

The last time we spoke, three years ago, in a small fortress on Silurian Isca, I was holding Madron hostage – or at least, I thought I was – trying to bargain for her fate with Ambrosius. We most certainly did not part on friendly terms; he barely let us out of his domain alive, and then only because my plan for the girl's future agreed with his own.

"Nonsense." He scoffs. "You did what you had to do. I wouldn't have done anything differently if I were in your place. What's done is done – and a long three years have passed since. Have your gods kept you well?"

"As well as anyone, lord *Dux*. Though…"

"What is it, boy?"

"I must say, I have grown weary of Cantiaca – and of the peace. I've been busy training my warriors and learning how to one day rule in my father's place. I was once sent with an embassy to Gaul, but after the adventures of three years ago, none of it can quell the yearning that burns in my heart."

Ambrosius chuckles. "Ah, youth! I forgot what it was like." He looks back to the city walls. "I don't think many here have grown weary of peace yet," he says. "Most of us remember more years of conflict than of calm, and know that the respite never lasts long enough. Still, I believe I can help you quench your yearning somewhat."

"With due respect, lord *Dux*, I have plenty of pirates and sea raiders to fight here in the East, and if I wanted more, I could've joined Audulf in Frisia."

He chuckles again and nods. "I figured as much. No, I don't need you fighting my wars for me – not yet, anyway… Mullo!"

He claps his hands. The old Legionnaire trots up to us from the front of the procession, bows to the *Dux* and turns to me.

"I have a message from Marcus," he says.

[28]

"And you couldn't have told it to me at Rutubi?" I ask.

"Marcus didn't want to distract you before the ceremony," Mullo says with a grin. "The message wasn't as important as ensuring the betrothal went smoothly. Now I can finally give it to you without worry."

"What is it, then?"

"He invites you and Ursula to a wedding. In Armorica."

"Armorica…? You mean – he's getting wedded to Ahes?"

Mullo nods.

"Finally! When?"

"On Saint James's Eve," he says.

"That's less than three months from now." I scratch my head. "I'm not sure if I can arrange transport to Armorica on such short notice."

"Come to Isca. We'll all be sailing from there. I'm sure we can find some room for you and your men."

"In that case, I will be there, you can count on that. I can't wait to tell Ursula and the others!"

The Song of the Tides

James Calbraith

CHAPTER II
THE LAY OF RHION

The promontory of the Dumnonian Isca rises in a tall, steep cliff over the river valley. The road linking the town with the bridge and the harbour descends down it like a waterfall of gravel. Loose paving stones, dislodged by centuries of rains and floods, have formed a pile at the bottom, which those in need of building stone have turned into a quarry of sorts; I wonder: how much of that ancient pavement served to raise the new Dumnonian seat of power at Dun Taiel?

That there is nothing to keep a Briton *Comes* occupied here is plain to see. Like so many former Legionnaire forts, most of the town was abandoned not long after the Roman soldiers departed. What is left is a ruined settlement within the compass of the broader wall, an oddly misshapen, elongated area surrounding the fortress itself – but there are fewer people living here than in some Iutish villages, all huddling around the stone church raised on the foundations of the old Forum.

Walking through the empty streets to our meeting place with Marcus, I recognise the shapes of the city's buildings – the great bath house, the *basilica*, the *Praetorium*; some still standing, but roofless and crumbling before the elements, others reduced to ruin and memory, traces of stone squares and rectangles of brick grown over with fern and grass. The Forum is now a graveyard, with fresh graves dug where food stalls once stood. Only the *Praetorium* is as tall now as it was when built: once overlooking the Forum, it now shares a courtyard entrance with the small church, built no doubt from stone taken from the baths and the *basilica*; but it, too, is

The Song of the Tides

for the most part empty now that the *Comes* has moved to his new capital.

A few guest rooms have been inserted into the eastern wing of the palace, where once the *Comes* and his family would have had their bedrooms. It is there that I find Marcus's warhorse, tied to a column of marble that once supported a *portico*. There is no door upon which I can knock – taken, no doubt, to Dun Taiel with the rest of the furniture and replaced by a cloth curtain.

"*Decurion?*" I call.

Presently, Marcus draws back the curtain. He's wearing the red tunic of a Roman officer, but over breeches of thick plaid wool, like a *druis* warrior.

"*Aetheling?*" He shields his eyes from the sun. "Is that really you?"

"Have I changed this much?"

"You've grown. And not just in height." He laughs, embracing me.

"The peace has been gentle to my waist, true," I admit. "Though I see you have not kept idle." I put my hand on his arm, then notice a wrapping around his thigh. "The Scots still trouble you?"

"It's nothing. A Saxon short sword."

"Saxons?" asks Ursula. "Here?"

[32]

"A small band of them we chased along the Belgian frontier."

"Must be Hrodha's men, still lost in these woods after all this time," Ursula guesses.

"We didn't ask their names or allegiance." Marcus grins. "Lady Ursula." He eyes her with surprise. "You wear woman's robes?"

She grins. "These are for the wedding," she says, and straightens the lines of her mantle. "I borrowed them from my mother."

"They lie on you beautifully. And this is…?"

He nods at Croha. I was reluctant to bring her, thinking her too young for the long journey, until Betula – the chief of my father's *Hiréd* and Croha's surrogate mother – reminded me she will soon be only a year younger than I was when I stowed away on Aegidius's *liburna*.

"She talks of nothing else but wishing to follow in yours and Ursula's footsteps," Betula told me, shaking her head. "You're her heroes ever since you've returned – more than I or Aeric ever were. You have to take her to see the world outside Cantia – she's waited long enough, and this looks like the perfect opportunity."

"Armorica is not as safe as Cantia," I reminded her. "The pirates could strike as we cross the Narrow Sea, the Bacauds could attack the town…"

"All of this could just as well happen here," Betula replied. "She has the same burning spirit within her as you and your father. If I keep her here for too long, she'll just run away one day, just as you did."

"One of the new, eager warriors I've been training to replace those lost in the battles three years ago," I introduce the girl to the *Decurion*. Croha, not as familiar with Imperial Latin as Ursula and I, only now realises we're talking about her, and stands to attention with her fist to her chest. "I left the rest of my men at the harbour."

"Who else has come?" Marcus asks.

"Ubba – and the two fishermen from Wecta. Acha and Raegen have little ones to take care of now, so they could only send their regards. The others –" It takes me a moment to remember Marcus wouldn't know Audulf, who chose three of his best new recruits to accompany him on our journey. We travelled light on a merchant's ship from Leman – this isn't supposed to be a war party. "– you'll get to know them better on the journey, I'm sure."

"And what of Seawine?"

"His days of travelling are over – he's content to stay in Cantia with his young recruits. There's only ten of us altogether. I didn't know how much room you could spare on your ship…"

"It's not *my* ship," Marcus laughs. "Graelon generously provided us with one of his. I'm sure it will be more than enough. After all, it's not like we're going to a war." He scratches his neck and looks to the sky; the sun is high, beaming fiercely on our heads. "But, you must be parched! Come in, I still have some *sicera* Ahes sent me with the ship…"

There's no mistaking it – this truly is one of Graelon's sleek warships, though a slightly smaller one than the *Maegwind* or *Seahorse* that we sailed on before. With our ten and Marcus's twenty, the quarters on, and under, the deck are impossibly cramped; there was no space even for our mounts. We're not supposed to be riding anywhere, as the wedding is to take part in the harbour of Gesocribate, so we left our ponies back in Isca. Thankfully, the journey is swift. On a good wind, we need to make only one, uneventful, stop in a tiny harbour on the island of Lenur, halfway between Dumnonia and Armorica.

"What took you so long?" I ask Marcus between bites of a dark Dumnonian bread. We eat a small *cena* on deck – there's no reason for us to disembark. There are no taverns or guesthouses on Lenur. "Did it really take you three years to convince Ahes to marry you?"

He laughs. "It wasn't her I had to convince – but her father. You know how little regard Graelon has for those of us who stayed in Britannia. He wanted to wed her to one of his Armorican friends, like Budic."

"Then what's changed?" asks Ursula.

"Ahes proved too stubborn." Marcus turns serious, and his eyes mist up. "For three years, she refused to even consider any other candidate to her hand. And Graelon might be a tough bastard, but he loves his daughter. She's all he's got left. And…" He picks up a piece of cured meat. "…my *Comes* aided us a little. He sent a few chests of our best tin and lead for Graelon's fleet to help convince him. It's not often that a husband needs to pay the dowry for the wife." He chuckles.

"Why would Urbanus do that?"

"An alliance with Graelon is worth almost any price for Dumnonia – and my wedlock to Ahes will secure it for a generation… Not that it was any consideration for either of us, of course."

"Of course." Ursula nods. She gives me a warm glance and moves closer, until her arm touches mine. "It's inspiring to see the light of love shine so brightly in these dark times."

In the morning, an hour after sailing from Lenur, I find Croha bent in half over the railing, spewing her breakfast into the sea below.

I pat her head and give her a wet towel to wipe her lips.

"Are you beginning to regret you came with us?" I ask. The waters seem calm to me, but the swell is noticeable, and we sail swiftly on the westerly breeze.

"Never, *aetheling*," she replies firmly.

"You should just call me Octa," I say. "We're practically brother and sister."

"Yes, *aetheling*," she says, nodding, then swiftly corrects herself. "Octa."

"You don't have much experience with ships, I'm guessing."

"I was brought to the Meon on a merchant's boat when I was a child – and then travelled with your father back to Cantia… But it was many years ago, and only a short journey. Nothing like this."

"You should go below the deck," I say. "You don't feel the swelling so much down there."

"I tried." She grimaces. "But I can't take the smell – the men…"

Her face turns grey-green again, but she bravely holds the retching back.

"It's not long now," I assure her. "Tonight we reach Armorica's northern coast, and then we hug the shore until Gesocribate."

"About that, *Hlaford*…"

I turn around to see Haering with his hand behind his neck.

"What is it?"

"Hleo and I wanted to tell you – we don't think we're going to Gesocribate."

I look to the sky. The sun is to our left.

"We're heading due south, aren't we?" I ask. "Isn't that the right way?"

The Song of the Tides

"We're going slightly west," Haering says. "I know these waters, and... We're moving away from where we're supposed to be."

"Maybe it's just the way the winds and currents are taking us," I guess. I know nothing about sailing – the ship's crew might as well be magicians, powering our vessel through prayer and the help of demons. But Hleo and Haering used to follow the shoals up and down the Narrow Sea when they were still fishermen at Wecta, and I refer to their knowledge of these waters.

"Maybe," says Haering, unconvinced. "But we should've waited for the easterly wind at Lenur. I can't think of a reason for us to be here, now." He glances at the filled-out mainsail and shakes his head.

"Get me the *Decurion*, just in case," I tell him. "And you, Croha – go find the ship's surgeon; he should have some root for you to chew on."

"Thank you, *aethel*... I mean, thank you, Octa."

By afternoon, it becomes clear even to me that there might be something to Haering's words. The Armorican coast looms a distant dark line in the haze of the horizon – to our starboard.

Marcus, Ursula and I find the ship's captain on the bow, staring at that dark line intently. He's startled by our sudden appearance.

"Y-yes?"

"Is this Armorica?" asks Marcus.

"Indeed."

"Then why are we sailing towards the east of it? Gesocribate lies on the western edge."

The captain steps away, his back to the railing, his hand reaching for the long knife at his side.

"It's only the prevailing winds, my lord," he stutters. "We will turn west as soon as we can."

"I've sailed these waters many times," says Marcus. "I've never heard of such a roundabout route."

"It's nothing to worry about, I assure you, my lords," the captain says. "There are good harbours on this coast, too. Should – should the wind keep us from turning today, we can just wait it out."

We leave him to his observations and walk away, but I can see Marcus remains unhappy with the captain.

"What do you think?" Ursula asks him.

"I don't trust him," the *Decurion* replies. "I know winds and currents can be treacherous in the Narrow Sea, but the wind is *not* pushing us eastwards. The helmsman is. This is deliberate." He rubs his chin. "I'll have my men ready, in case of trouble."

"What trouble do you expect?" I ask. "Pirates?"

The Song of the Tides

"Perhaps. He might be taking us into a trap… Or he might truly know something about the winds that I don't. He *is* an experienced captain – I've only ever been a passenger."

By the time the sun touches the horizon, it's clear we're not being led into the pirates' lair – they wouldn't dare attack us this close to the shore. Still, the captain's plan remains a mystery. The wind dies down for the evening, and the ship moves by the power of the dozen oarsmen labouring under the deck. Against the receding tide, we head for a smattering of land, too small and remote to be part of the mainland.

We reach the entrance to a shallow cove, some half a mile from shore. There's no harbour here – only what looks like a tiny fishing hamlet, sheltered beyond a mass of yellow and red rock, shattered and cracked by waves and wind: a few round huts of rough stone, topped with reed thatch. Before long, the tide ebbs away, leaving the ship surrounded by mud and reefs. The stench of seaweed and rotten mussels hits my nostrils like a fist.

Marcus waits no longer. He grabs the captain by the tunic and presses him to the railings.

"What is this place?" Marcus demands from the captain.

"It's… just an island. It has no name."

"What are we doing here?"

I tap the *Decurion*'s shoulder; he turns to see the ship's crewmates surrounding us in a tight ring. They're all armed with long knives, hatchets and working tools. The tallest of them, with the muscles and demeanour of a warrior, rather than a sailor, points at us with a short, double-edged sword.

"We have orders to stay the night here," he says.

"*Orders?* Whose orders?" demands Marcus.

We have no weapons on us – there's no reason to carry them around the ship. But behind the crewmen, I can see the *equites* and the Iutes gather, anxiously, a few of them brandishing their swords.

I put my hand on Marcus's shoulder. "We can kill them all," I whisper, "but who's going to steer the ship then?"

"I just want to know what's going on," he replies. "What's Graelon playing at?"

"I don't know anything else," the captain says, spreading his arms helplessly. "It's only for one night. In the morning, we sail straight for Gesocribate."

Marcus frowns. "I don't like this. I don't like this one bit. Why the delay?"

"Something must have happened in Worgium," I guess, unconvinced. "Maybe Graelon needs more time to prepare."

"The wedding's not in a few weeks yet. He'd have plenty of time to prepare." He rubs his chin. "And why are these men so hostile?" He looks towards the shore, quickly disappearing in the gloom. "It's not far," he says. "We could always try to swim there, if we have to."

"Not in the dark."

The Song of the Tides

He lets go of the captain and we wait for the ship's crew to stand down. Once again, there's nothing left to do but wait until morning, hoping that things will be looking brighter then.

Audulf shakes me awake. Immediately, I notice something's terribly wrong. The ship's rolling on the waves and listing heavily to port. The *equites* and the Iutes are running about on the deck, grasping at the ropes, and throwing crates and *amphorae* overboard.

"Marcus and Ursula?" I ask.

"At the helm," Audulf replies.

I rush towards the stern, avoiding the load sliding down the wet deck. Glancing over the side, I realise we're no longer at anchor; the fishing village is more than a mile away now, and instead, the strong tide is pushing us towards a forest of sharp, jagged rocks on the edge of the cove.

Marcus, Drustan and a couple other *equites* are holding on to the steering oar, struggling to turn us away from the reefs. Ursula looks overboard, shouting directions to them.

"What happened?" I ask. "Where's the crew?"

"Gone!" replies Marcus. "Only the oarsmen remain. They're the only ones helping us keep this thing afloat."

"What do you mean – *gone*? How? When?"

"Some other boat must have picked them up at night," says Ursula. "But not before they hacked holes in the hull. We're taking water fast."

"How did we not notice it? Didn't you leave a watch?"

"Whoever came to help them, killed two of my men," Marcus snarls. "How about we solve that mystery after we survive!"

I look around for a way to help – I notice Hleo and Haering struggling to hold onto one of the two great ropes hanging from the spar. The other rope flails freely. I run to grab it. It slips away, cutting my hands like a spear blade. I grasp again, more firmly this time, and plant my feet on the deck.

"What now?" I cry to the two fishermen.

"Pull towards us," Haering cries back. "Hoist it up!"

It seems an impossible task. The breeze fills out the sail and keeps tearing the rope from my hands. One of the *equites* grabs the rope's end behind me and together we manage to flatten the cloth until it flutters in vain, then, slowly, pull it up so that it no longer pushes us towards the land. The ship heaves and rolls even more to port; the reefs ahead start to disappear to the starboard – but not fast enough.

The disaster unravels with agonising sluggishness. With everyone on board trying their best to help steer the ship away from the reef, we manage to slowly rotate the vessel's side towards them, instead of the bow – but the tide proves too strong, and we don't know how to turn the ship away from it. At last, the waves grind us against the sharp rocks;

The Song of the Tides

the jagged edges tear the wood apart like parchment, water gushes in. I hear the screams of the poor oarsmen, still struggling to keep us afloat, drowning under the deck, helpless; only two of them emerge out alive, gasping. We hold on to the ropes and the rails as the waves drag the wreck from the rocks only to throw us again, a hundred feet closer to land.

"We have to jump!" I cry. "Swim ashore! We'll have more chance this way!"

Marcus and Ursula nod in agreement. The *Decurion* shouts orders to his men while I gather my Iutes around me, even as the ship – or what's left of it – crashes into the rocks for the third time.

"Take only your weapons," I order the men. "Throw away everything that can weigh you down. Remember your training – don't be afraid; it's a shorter way than across to Tanet."

Croha is the first to leap into the cold waters. For a moment, she disappears under the surface, and my heart sinks with her; when her head pops out again, she's already a good hundred feet away from the wreck.

I wait until all my men are in the sea. Ursula is the last one.

"Too bad we didn't take our ponies," she says, staring at the dark, churning water below.

"They would've all drowned below deck," I reply. "We'll have to manage without them. Now go, before we're crushed by the waves!"

[44]

"Race to the shore?" she says with a grin.

"Sure. I'll beat you as always!"

The fishing hamlet is empty when we reach it – soaked through, shivering with cold and with our clothes torn to shreds on the gravel but, miraculously, all alive.

"They must've fled when they saw the ship yesterday," I guess. "What do we do?"

"The huts have no doors," notes Marcus. "And they're dry inside. I don't know about you, but I'm going to try to find one with a still smouldering hearth."

The place he finds stinks of rotten fish and is crawling with all manner of small creatures, but the embers are still burning, and soon we're able to hang our clothes around the blazing hearth to dry.

"What do you think happened over there?" I ask when my teeth finally stop chattering.

"Graelon doesn't want me coming to the wedding, that much is certain," he replies.

"But then, why go through all this trouble?" asks Ursula. "Why send a ship for us in the first place, only to abandon us here?"

"He didn't just want me away – he wanted me *dead*," replies Marcus grimly. "And in what looked like an accident.

Why?" He shrugs. "I don't know. But first, we need to find out where *here* is."

Once we're all dry and warm, we gather at the beach in plain sight, unarmed, and wait for the fishermen to gather enough courage to return to their huts. Before long, they appear – as if out of nowhere. The island is so full of rocky outcrops, copses of dwarf birch and hazel and steep dunes that it could hide an entire town's worth of people, and I'm beginning to wonder if the ship's captain and his crew are still here somewhere, hiding in some scrub.

"Do you think they even speak Latin here?" I wonder.

"We'll soon see. You, there!" Marcus calls one who looks like the village elder. He approaches, half-bent in a bow.

"What do they call this place?" the *Decurion* asks. "Where are we?"

The elder replies in a mumbling, barely legible Vulgar. He needs to repeat the answer three times before we understand him.

"You're on Laurea."

I look to Marcus. He shakes his head. "Never heard of it. Do you have a master?"

"This be Budic's land."

"Budic!" Marcus smacks his fist in his palm. "That bastard! I knew we hadn't seen the last of him."

"At least we now know we're not far from Graelon's lands," says Ursula.

"Wait a moment —" I ask "— if this is a fishing village, where are your boats?"

"Our — what?"

"Boats. *Naui*." I imitate paddling.

"Budic's men take," he replies. "And burn. We're hungry." He mimes putting food in his mouth.

"We're hungry, too," Marcus replies with a scowl. He turns to his men. "Go back to the rocks," he commands them. "See if the sea didn't throw out some of the ship's supplies."

As the *equites* disappear in search of food, I suggest to Marcus that we climb to the top of the tallest nearby hill, to get the lay of our land.

"We can't be far from the mainland," I say, "if Budic's men were here."

He looks up to the summit, rising some half a mile to the south, over a dense pine grove, and winces. "They might still be here, hiding. I would rather stay with my men and wait, in case they come to check if anyone survived the wreckage."

"Then I'll go. Ursula, Ubba and Audulf — come with me."

"Let me go with you too, *aetheling*."

The Song of the Tides

Croha steps forward, pressing her *seax* to her chest. Once back on dry land, colour returned to her cheeks and flame to her eyes. I recognise the weapon in her hand, with some surprise, as one of the blades my mother wrought – the girl must have brought it with her from Wecta.

"Fine." I nod. "I don't think we'll be in any danger here, but stay vigilant in any case. And I told you before – it's Octa, not *aetheling*."

We reach the top after a short hike through the dark wood and emerge onto a sun-blasted heath glade. A lone pine, twisted by the winds, grows in the middle. Before I say anything, Croha leaps onto it and climbs to the top.

"What do you see?" I ask.

She gazes in every direction, shielding her eyes from the midday sun.

"I can't see the mainland," she calls back. "All I see is marshes, mud, rocks – and another island to the south." She notices something in the distance and leans forward, dangerously.

"Careful!" I cry.

"There's a causeway – or a ford," she replies, heedless of my warning. "We should be able to wade through. It can't be more than a hundred feet across."

"We were only supposed to climb up here," says Ursula.

"We were supposed to get the lay of the land," I reply. "We have to check that causeway."

I reach out to help Croha down the last few feet. She leaps down and lands softly in the ferns.

"Follow me!" she exclaims, and rushes down the southern slope.

"Wait —"

There is a rugged beauty to the rocks scattered across the mudflats on the island's southern shore. Covered in cracks and wrinkles like the forehead of an old woman, they seem to grow out of the sea floor like some strange, colourful flowers: yellow, pink, red, with bands of green and blue marking the line of high tide. I find Croha on the beach, struck into awed silence by the view.

"You've never seen anything like it," I say. The rocks in Cantia, if they at all appear from under the grass, are grey or chalk white, and form sheer cliffs and jagged edges, not these impossible blooms.

"My father once told me of a beach on Wecta where each grain of sand was of a different hue," she replies. "But I thought it was just a story."

"These may well be the same rocks, pounded into dust by waves," I say, nodding. "Wecta is only across the Narrow Sea from here."

"This is no time to be admiring the views," says Ursula, breathlessly after catching up to us. "Where's that ford?"

The Song of the Tides

Croha points to a narrow strait between our island and the other, larger one. She was right – we can wade across with ease; though, if we don't return before the tide, we'll have to swim back.

"Look." I point to the other side. "A dirt road. That means there must be another settlement here."

"One that might be crawling with Budic's men," warns Ubba.

"I take it this Budic is not a friend of yours," says Audulf.

"He's almost as bad as Wortimer," I tell him. "The lot of them are, here. Ahes is about the only decent one of them all. We'd best be careful."

The dirt road bears no cart tracks or hoof tracks, so if there is a village here it must be as small as the one on the northern isle. We follow it for another half a mile, before entering a dense wood.

"I smell fire," says Croha.

I draw my sword and nod at the others to do the same, quietly. We follow the scent until we reach a secluded cove with a broad beach of colourful pebbles – and six men, naked, sitting around a campfire and waiting for their clothes to dry on the stones. Their weapons – long knives, clubs and hatchets – lie beside them.

Croha, wanting to take a closer look, takes a step too far and slips on the pebbles. She slides down onto the beach and lands on her bottom. The men leap up, grabbing their weapons. "Audulf – right, Ubba – left. Don't kill them," I call out an order and run out of the woods with Ursula. I rush at the first of the men, head down, and throw him to the ground. The one to my right strikes with the axe; Ursula parries it with ease. The strangers are weary, and poor fighters. I overpower another one, twisting his arm behind his back. Ursula grasps the third and throws him over her head in a deft wrestling move.

To my left, I glance Audulf grab his sword by the blade and whirl it like a mace. He dodges a knife thrust and smashes his foe over the head with the pommel. The two remaining men assail Ubba, pinning him to the rock. He's in trouble – his foes wield short swords and use them with some skill – but neither I nor Ursula can help him, busy with our own three enemies. I kick my first foe to keep him from getting up, then grab the other by the arm and spin him around so the two fall over each other. I reach for the knife in my boot, hoping to throw it in the back of one of Ubba's opponents, but before I can do that, Croha charges with a wild cry, waving her sword over her head; her blade falls on the shoulder of one of the naked men, slipping down his collarbone. The wound is slight, but it distracts him enough for Ubba to cut the other man on the shoulder, then on the thigh; as he falls to his knees, Ubba and Croha grab the first one by the shoulders and together smash his head on the rock. He slides down with blood spurting from his brow.

"*Aetheling*, look!" Ubba cries. He picks up one of the drying garments: it's the torn mantle of the Martinians.

I kneel on the chest of the man under me and press the blade to his neck.

"You're Bacauds? Bastards!"

The Song of the Tides

He raises his hands. "Please – only those two are –" He points to Ubba's foes. "– we took them in… They're just fugitives like us."

"Fugitives? You mean from Budic?"

"Budic?" He frowns. "No – we're running away from the *Capillati*."

He's a local – speaking the same mumbling variety of Vulgar as the fishermen in the village. I let him go and stand up. I order the others to bring all six before me. They're trembling, seawater still dripping from their limbs.

"Sit down. Give them their breeches," I command. I wait until they put on their clothes. The two Bacauds are still bleeding from their wounds; I set them aside and tell Ubba to keep an eye on them, then turn back to the one I spoke with first.

"What do you mean, the *Capillati*?" I ask. The word is not the name of some new tribe – it's an old Imperial term for the "long-haired" warriors from the barbarian north. "What are you all doing here?"

"Looking for a safe place," he replies. "The *Capillati* burned our homes, villages… killed or captured our families…"

He stops to sneeze.

"What's your name?" I ask him.

"Rhion."

"These *Capillati*, Rhion… What do they look like?"

He glances to Ubba and Audulf. "Some look like your men there… But bearded and curly haired. They are many. A whole army. Horsemen, spearmen… They say they only hunt the Bacauds and the bandits – but they destroy everything in their path."

"What about the cities and the houses of nobles?"

"They say the nobles are the ones who brought them here," Rhion replies bitterly.

Looking closer, I notice that his right arm is bulging with sword muscles, he bears several deep scars on his upper body – and his shoulders are marked with indentations left by tight bronze armbands.

I take Ursula aside and speak to her in Iutish.

"A Saxon warband?" I ask. "Here?"

"The Briton nobles would never hire Saxon mercenaries," she says. "They despise fair-hairs."

"We don't know if he's telling the truth. Or that he even knows it."

"He knows more than he's telling. Look at him – he's a warrior, not a peasant." I glance at the other men. "Whoever these strangers are, they must have something to do with us being stranded here. Maybe Graelon did us a favour after all…"

The Song of the Tides

Audulf comes up to us. "I've checked that boat. It's in bad shape, but I think it could manage ferrying all ten of us – one way."

He points to the dark line of land some two miles to the south.

"Is this where you came from?" I ask Rhion. "Or yet another island?"

"That's Broom Point," he says. "On the mainland."

"I don't suppose you know how far we are from a place called Worgium?"

"I don't – but a day's march from Broom Point is the old stone road that can take you anywhere you want."

"What are you thinking?" asks Ursula. "We can't abandon Marcus and his men."

"We're not going to – we're going to find out what's going on and get help. Croha, come with me back to the village. The rest of you, stay here and prepare that boat. I want us on the other side before nightfall!"

Upon our return to the fishing hamlet, we're welcomed by a handful of bloodied corpses, strewn at the entrance. One of the oarsmen is lying there, too, pierced with a blade through his back.

"Looks like you were right," I say to Marcus as he wipes fresh blood from his sword. I lean over one of the attackers. He looks like the men described by Rhion: long, fair hair, a short, scraggly beard and a thick moustache, light armour, and a short, single-edged sword, still in his hand.

"They fought well," says Marcus, rubbing a cut in his shoulder with a wince. "But they're neither Britons nor Armoricans. Who are they?"

"I don't know," I reply. "They're of no tribe I'm familiar with. And I don't think these ones came after *us*."

I tell him of our meeting with Rhion and show him the five men I brought with me from the beach. "Tie up these two." I point to the wounded Bacauds. "But the others can be trusted, I think. They've been trapped here just as we are."

"How did they get here?"

"They have one small boat," I reply. "I want to use it to find help. We could try to row back for the rest of you, but I don't know how long it will hold. It's –"

"No." Marcus raises his hand. "We'll stay here. If anyone spots us on the mainland, Graelon will know I survived. I'd rather give him a surprise, at least until I really know what's going on. We've gathered enough food to last us a few days. Find out what's going on here, then come back for us as soon as you can."

"You won't have to wait long for the rescue, I promise."

"I know I can count on you, *aetheling*."

The Song of the Tides

CHAPTER III
THE LAY OF WENELIA

"These are no Saxons," says Audulf.

"And no mere bandits," I note. I point out the long coat of mail hanging on the rack by the largest of tents, and a stack of gleaming spears beside it. I spot a few large shields outside the tents: oval, painted red and white, marked with dragon and raven heads, and strange runes that look like Greek letters.

These "strangers" made no effort to hide themselves from the enemies, which tells me they must believe the area around them thoroughly subdued. This is a small detachment, a mere dozen or so riders, guarding a crossroad – the Roman road to Worgium and a dirt track from Broom Point – while the main warband is busy slaughtering innocents elsewhere.

As we followed the track, guided by the reluctant Rhion, we passed several farms and hamlets, burnt to smouldering ruins, the people all slain or captured. It reminded me of the part of Gaul through which the Huns have marched, similarly dotted with monuments to the violence, plunder and destruction wrought onto a defenceless land and powerless people. Only here, the enemy did not defeat a defending army before unleashing their destructive power – if what Rhion tells us is true, these nameless warriors are in league with the new lords of Armorica…

"Should we wait until they're gone?" asks Ubba.

"Who knows how long that will take," I reply. "Besides, we could use the horses. It will take days to reach Worgium on foot."

"You want to attack them?"

"Why not? There's ten of us and twelve of them. I like those odds."

"Only us four have any experience in battle," says Ursula.

"I bet these aren't the enemy's best warriors, either," I say. "Or they wouldn't be left here to guard this lonely outpost."

As we wait and observe the men in the camp, Croha, sent to watch the eastern road, returns with news of two more riders approaching.

"They have a prisoner," she reports.

"A prisoner?" I frown. "Is this what they are waiting for?"

This is an unwelcome development. Two more riders turn the odds against us — now we have to wait until they're gone, or try to find another way around. They soon appear on the crossroads; they're in no hurry: they drag their barely conscious prisoner, tied between the two mounts by her hands, her face beaten and bloodied.

As they arrive, a man walks out of the large tent, dressed only in plain green breeches. He's tall and slim, his body built of taut muscles, strong sinews and deep scars. He says something to the two riders, and they throw the prisoner into the dirt before him. Even their tongue is unfamiliar. I grasp only a few words, sounding similar to Frankish, but softer, rounder, rustling like wind in the trees. It is far too gentle a tongue to be spoken by such brutes.

The chief lifts the woman by her chin and asks her a question in rough Vulgar.

"Where are they?"

She spits blood in his face. He smacks her and repeats his question. She grunts in reply. The chieftain barks an order at the riders; to my relief, they salute him and turn back. He slaps the woman again and throws her to his men. The warriors tie her to a stake and strip her from what few rags she's wearing. I notice the woman is with child – not heavily, yet, but noticeably so.

Rhion tenses beside me. He rises up – I grab him before he can betray our position.

"Calm down. What is it?"

"That's Wenelia, from my village," he says.

"These people are looking for you?" asks Ursula. "You didn't mention that."

"I don't know why they care so much to find us," he replies. "They slaughtered everyone else… What difference does six more make?"

"You got away," says Ursula. "Maybe they're afraid you'll get help from somewhere."

"There is no help," Rhion says grimly. "We're all alone against them."

"Not anymore," I say. I draw the sword. "Croha, how good are you with those flying axes?"

The girl grins. "Betula says I will soon surpass her."

I raise my eyebrow. "That's quite a boast."

"I'd show you if we had the time."

"You'll have to show me now. *He* is your target." I point to the chief.

She twists her lips. "I'd need to get really close. He's a lanky one."

I nod. "I'll mark him for you."

"Please, hurry," Rhion whispers with trembling lips, watching the enemy warriors torment Wenelia. The fear and fury in his eyes tell me the woman is more to him than just a fellow villager.

"Audulf, get your recruits and line up on the road," I order. "Get their attention. Croha, stay with me. Ursula will lead the rest. We don't have much time – we don't know when those two will return."

"Let me fight," says Rhion. "I want to kill at least one."

I glance at his arms once again. There's no doubt that he fought before, but can we really rely on him in this battle?

I give him my knife.

"We won't be saving you if anything goes wrong."

"I know," he says with a determined nod. "Just hurry up."

Audulf's group rushes out of the wood; they shuffle towards the camp as if they are all injured and weary, hiding their swords behind their backs. As soon as the chief of the *Capillati* notices them on the road, he calls on his warriors. I count them as they emerge from their tents.

"Eleven," I whisper to Ursula. "One less than the horses."

"One may be injured. Or out on patrol."

"No matter. Now at least we're equal in numbers."

The chief eyes Audulf with suspicious confusion. At last, he decides the Iutes, whoever they are, have got too close to the camp and sends five of his men to get them. The warriors take no chances: they pick up their spears and shields before approaching Audulf cautiously. The chief himself orders a servant to bring him the mail shirt and helmet.

"Now!" I cry.

Ursula, Ubba and the two Wecta fishermen run out of their hiding place. Hleo and Haering are no longer the timid pony handlers that they were on our expedition to Britannia; they never returned to their island and chose instead to spend the last three years training with my other warriors. They showed little skill with the *seax* and the spear; as they run behind Ursula, screaming, each one is waving a different weapon – Hleo a large axe, Haering – a heavy spiked club.

At the same moment, Audulf and his three recruits draw their swords and charge at the warriors before them.

"Rhion, get your woman off that rack," I order. "Croha – wait here and make your axe ready."

"How will I know when to strike?"

"You'll know."

I catch only the briefest of glances to my left and right, to make sure Ursula and Audulf are engaged with the enemy on either side of the camp. I have to trust in their skills, and those of the men I helped train. I need to focus all my attention on my own adversary: the chief of the band. In his mail coat and steel helmet, with a long *spatha* sword and a large shield, painted with the strange runes – and, I notice with surprise, a silver *chrismon* – he seems a formidable opponent; when he notices me and raises the sword above his head with a roar, I realise I'm putting my life in the inexperienced hands of Croha. There's no way I can possibly defeat this man on my own.

With all the other warriors busy fighting Ursula and Audulf, the only man left in the camp is the torturer, still busy cutting Wenelia's skin when we emerge from the forest. Rhion rushes past me and runs towards him with a pained wail; I have no hope he will survive this – it will be a feat if he manages to distract the enemy long enough to keep him off my back. I point my sword at the chief and shout a challenge

— in Frankish, hoping to confuse him further. This works for a split second as he stares at me with a frown.

"Who *are* you people?" he replies to my challenge in good Frankish, before charging at me with the shield. I block it with my sword, holding it in two hands, and duck to avoid his blade, slashing the air where my head just was. I push back and try to hit him around the shield — right side, then left side; he strikes again. Our blades clash. He bashes me with the shield. I roll with the bash, to lessen the blow, and spin around. On the way back, I hack with full force.

I may have grown pudgy over these past three years, as Marcus noticed, but I also worked on my muscles. Losing strength too swiftly or being unable to execute a blow fierce enough to fell an enemy with one thrust, had caused me plenty of trouble in the campaigns in Gaul and Wened, and I made sure to train until I could splinter a thick wooden board in two with a single strike.

But the chief's shield is bound in iron, and made of tough wood, and he knows how to take my blow and turn into a glance. The shield cracks, but does not break; a shard of metal flies from my blade. I will not win through strength here. He strikes again, overhead; I parry, but can't block the shield at the same time, and the metal boss hits me in the chest.

"Where did these serfs find you?" the chief asks, waiting for me to catch my breath. "Graelon didn't warn us about any warriors in this region."

"Then you *do* work for him!"

The Song of the Tides

He laughs and takes up the battle stance again, with the thrusting sword resting on the edge of the shield. I lower myself to take on the next charge, and glance to my left to check on Audulf. One of his recruits lies, bleeding, on the road, but so are two of the enemy. Before I can look to Ursula, the chief rushes forth, certain he will bring me down this time.

I step aside, whirl the sword until its tip points downwards and stab him in the foot through the leather boot. The edge of the shield strikes my shoulder and sends me spinning. The chief yelps and struggles with my sword – the blade digs deep into a crack between the paving stones. I grab his shield and try to wrestle it from his grasp. He pushes away; I pull; the sword in his foot gives way and we tumble down, with him on top. He grasps the blade of his sword in both hands and puts it to my neck.

"I'll ask one last time," he hisses. "What Hell have you come from, heathen?"

Now would be a good time, Croha… I think, desperately, and close my eyes.

I hear the flutter of a flying axe; it glances the chief on the shoulder. He looks back, annoyed at the distraction. I gather my strength, grab him by the arms and try to lift him up. The chief frowns and grunts as he pushes me back. With a heave and a roar, I press and kick upwards, but he doesn't budge. Just then, a blurry shape smashes his side. The chief's grip on me slackens. I throw him off and roll away. I see him reach for the man who just assaulted him: it's Rhion, covered in blood and unarmed, but seething with fury and vengeance, snarling like an angry wildcat. He grabs the chief tightly around the chest and, heedless of the blows falling on his head and back, turns him around, just in time for Croha's second axe to hit the chief – and this time, it lands straight between his shoulder blades.

He grunts again, this time in pain, and falls to his knees. He flails his hands at his back, trying to tear the axe out. I grab my sword from the ground and, with a mighty blow, just as I practised all those months on straw dummies, I sever his head.

I grab the head by the hair and throw it into the middle of the fight between Ursula's group and four of the enemies. Seeing their chief dead saps their strength and attention momentarily. Within a few blows of the axe and club, they're all brought down; Ursula and Ubba finish them off with quick thrusts. The three remaining warriors on Audulf's side, seeing this, throw their spears and try to run for the horses, but Audulf's young recruits, lightly armed and with no armour, are faster; their knives glint silver in the sun and, with each glint, a red flower blooms in the backs of the enemy.

"Rhion!"

I hurry to the Armorican's side. He lies sprawled across the chief's headless body. I can instantly tell his wounds are too grievous for him to survive. I look at the torturer – he lies dead by his device in a pool of blood. In his vengeful frenzy, Rhion must have stabbed him a dozen times with the small knife I gave him.

Rhion gurgles bloody spittle. "Wenelia –" he rasps.

The woman lies on the ground beside the slain warrior, but I can't tell if she, too, is dead or just unconscious.

"She's safe," I lie. I put the knife back in his hands – its blade broken on the torturer's bones – cross his arms on his chest and wait for him to breathe his last breath.

Ursula and Audulf stand above me. "They're all dead," says Audulf. "Too bad – I was hoping they'd tell us who they are, and what they're doing here."

"It's fine," I say, standing up. "I think I already know."

"We lost Picga," says Audulf. The youngest of the three recruits lies on his back, his arms thrown apart, a gaping hole in his chest. "He threw himself on the spear. Saved my life."

We have no time for burials or mourning. I help Audulf drag the young warrior's body into the roadside and lay it beside that of Rhion. We cover them with leaves and dirt while Ursula whispers a short prayer.

"Get whatever you need from the camp," I order the men. "Weapons, food… Be quick about it."

"What do we do with her?" asks Ursula.

Wenelia is still alive – though barely; she's slowly coming to her senses. Croha puts a tunic and cloak over her naked, bruised body.

"Put her on your horse," I say. "We'll leave her at the next village."

"If there are any villages left."

We finish packing; I strip the chief from his mail coat and try it on – it's too tight for me, but I take it anyway, hoping to find a blacksmith that will adjust it to my size. I take his lance and shield and strap them to the saddle of the largest of the twelve horses.

"Be careful," I say to the recruits. "There's still one man unaccounted for. He may have gone to get help."

The two youths nod in silence. They are both grey-faced and glum. Blood of the enemies has dried in dark stains on their clothes, and clumps in their hair.

"This was their first fight," Audulf says quietly. "Their first kills, and the first death of a comrade."

"I know," I reply. "I'll talk to them later. For now, we must go."

I mount up and look at the remains of the camp. The campfire is still smouldering, so I order the youths to put the tents to the torch.

"Raze it like they razed those villages," I say, hoping the act of vengeful destruction will lift their spirits. I glance to the east and notice a movement in the distance. "But hurry while you're at it," I add.

"You said you knew who they were," Ursula says when we slow down to a trot a few miles west of the battle site. The road turns southwards now, which matches what I remember of Armorica's map. On horseback, we should reach the town tomorrow – not that I know yet what we will do when we get there. If what I think is true, none of us will be welcome in Graelon's domain.

The Song of the Tides

"It's something that chieftain said before he died," I say. "He called us *heathens*. And he wore a *chrismon* on his shield."

"That's it?"

"They are fair-hairs, of that there is no doubt. But they are Christian, and they wield Roman arms. And that writing on their shields – I remember now where I saw it. A Gaulish merchant's ledger in Dubris."

"Who are they, then?"

"Goths."

"*Goths?*" she exclaims. There is a hint of terror in her voice that I rarely hear, and I'm reminded that to those of the Briton nobles who were aware of the happenings on the Continent, the name of the Goths strikes as much fear as that of the Huns. A generation ago, it was the Goths who ravaged Italia and sacked Rome, marking the culmination of the catastrophe that ended with the Imperial troops leaving Britannia forever.

Since then, they have been variously allies and enemies of the Empire; they forced their way into Gaul and were allowed to settle in its south, and in Hispania. The last time we heard of them was during our adventure in Gaul, when they threatened Imperator Maiorianus's flank in his campaign against the usurper Avitus – but they were beaten back soon after our victory at Trever and, as far as I know, have kept quiet ever since.

"Must be," I say. "Of all the nearby barbarian peoples Graelon could have recruited as his allies, only the Goths have been Christian for long enough to scoff at other barbarians for their heathenry. And they will be looking for somewhere to expand after Maiorianus pushed them out in the South."

"There can't be many of them," she says, "or they would have overrun the entire province."

"A small cohort, perhaps," I say. "To secure the area for a future conquest… Or maybe it's something else. There's hardly enough here worth conquering for the Britons – I can't imagine Armorica alone would be a prize worth dying for to the Goths." I rub my chin. "There must be something else."

"And what does any of it have to do with poor Marcus and Ahes's wedding?"

"We'll find out soon enough."

We ride undisturbed for the next several hours. The Goths must have wreaked their destruction in another direction, for apart from a small burnt-down hamlet an hour from the crossroad, the villages we pass on our way to Worgium are intact. The reason soon becomes apparent when I decide to find some family in whose care we could leave Wenelia.

"We don't want her here," says the woman in the first house, brusquely. She speaks with a Briton accent, rather than the local variety of Vulgar. I now realise that hers is the only speech I've been hearing in the villages we have passed. "Take her back where you found her."

"Her whole village was destroyed," I say. "She has nowhere to go."

"Good." The woman's voice cuts like cold steel. "They should have killed her, too. And cut out that Bacaud bastard from her belly. We don't need any more of their spawn."

I glance at her house. Like all the others in the village, it's built in local style, rather than in the Briton manner. There are scorch marks around the door, and the thatch is new, still fresh, replaced with hides at the rear. The entire village around us bears signs of recent destruction. A hut on the outskirts is burnt to the ground.

She looks over my shoulder, to where Audulf and the rest of the Iutes are standing, waiting.

"Who are you, anyway?" she asks suspiciously. "Are these men with you?"

"They're our guard," I reply, not for the first time blessing my mother for giving me the features that allow me to pass for a Briton to people like these villagers. "We've only just arrived from Cantia – we're heading for Worgium."

The suspicious frown doesn't fade from her face, but she turns it into a false-looking smile. "Ah, you're going for the princess's wedding, no doubt?"

"Just so." I nod.

"Well, then, maybe they'll take care of her in Worgium," she says. "You'll find no Bacaud-lovers here."

With that, she slams the door in our face. All over the village, the hut doors shut around us.

"Are they all like this here?" asks Audulf.

"I told you they were worse than Wortimer," I tell him. "What do we do now?"

"We must take that poor woman with us to Worgium," says Ursula. "Maybe someone will have mercy on her there."

"And I think it'll be best if we avoid *all* villages from now on," I add.

Eolh and Deor, the two surviving youths, are about the same age as Croha; like her – and like me – they're of the new generation of Iutes, born outside the Isle of Tanet, not knowing the squalor and hardship our people experienced before the Cants allowed us to settle on their land. Even the war with Wortimer is only a distant, dark memory. In the ten years that have passed since the battle of Eobbasfleot, they would have had few opportunities to see a man killed. If they lived on the coast, they might have witnessed a raid from the Frankish pirates or the Pictish slavers; if their families had settled near Andreda, they may have seen the aftermath of a forest bandits' ambush. But Eolh and Deor were both born and raised near Rutubi, in the shadow of my father's royal mead hall, protected by the mighty walls of the old Roman fortress, and the closest they could have come to violence in battle until now would have been if they'd suffered an injury during their warrior training.

I gather them and Croha around the campfire. I give them a flask of strong ale I picked up in the Goth chief's tent, and then I wait for the liquor to start working its magic.

"You did well," I say when I see their cheeks are sufficiently flushed. "All of you."

The Song of the Tides

I feel odd starting this speech. I didn't need to do this after the first battle in Gaul with my dozen Iute riders. But they were all older – older than me, older than these youths; they knew a harsh life, life of danger and violence. They all survived Wortimer's War, slaver raids, some even fought at Crei. None of them looked up to me as an older figure of authority, like these three. What do I even tell them? What would my father tell them?

"Croha," I start. "You killed a Goth chieftain. Some warriors go through their entire life without achieving a feat like that."

"A fortunate shot," she says with a shy grin. "Poor Rhion set him up for me like a target board."

"*Audentes Fortuna iuvat,*" I say.

"I – I don't understand."

Of course – she didn't have the classical education I had under Bishop Fastidius. Betula only made sure to train her how to wield a sword and throw an axe, not how to speak Imperial Latin.

"*Fortune favours the audacious,*" I say. "It's a Roman saying."

"*Wodan rewards the bold,*" says Eolh, staring into the fire. "Something my father used to say."

"Was your father a warrior, then?" I ask.

He nods. "He defended Robriwis from Wortimer. Wounded at Eobbasfleot."

"He'll be proud of you, Eolh. You fought like a true Iute warrior. Sword against spear is the most difficult battle you can have on foot."

"I know. I saw Picga's stomach skewered like a wild boar on a spit roast."

I put my hand on his shoulder. "He died a warrior's death. He's dining with Wodan right now." I look to the dark sky. "We all die, sooner or later. A fisherman drowns in the sea. A farmer cuts himself with the sickle and dies of wound rot. A hunter gets gorged by a wild boar. You and I chose a warrior's life. This is how we die – Wodan willing."

He nods again. "I understand, *aetheling*."

"But today, we are all alive. And we will live a few days more at least, that much I guarantee." I stand up. "Tomorrow we reach Worgium. There will be no fighting there, only warm food and good bed at an inn."

But there is no bed or warm food at Worgium. The town is shut – as much as a place like Worgium, a sprawling mess of huts and tenements without a wall, can be. As soon as I notice the soldiers guarding a blockade on the approach from the east, I order my men to turn around and get off the main road into the woods.

"Something tells me it's not a good idea for us all to enter Worgium," I say. "A band of fair-hairs will only draw attention. Ursula and I will go alone."

"Those guards might recognise us," says Ursula.

"It's been three years," I reply.

"Graelon could have told them to be on the lookout for anyone who boarded that ship. Why else would he put up that blockade?"

"We have to risk it. We're the only ones who can speak the language, and know how to find Ahes."

"Let me go with you," Wenelia says weakly.

The woman woke up for the first time this morning. She wasn't badly wounded – under Croha's and Ursula's care, most of her injuries had already begun to heal. Worse were the wounds of the mind. She wouldn't start talking for several hours. When she finally spoke, her first word was "*Rhion*".

"He died fighting for you," Ursula explained.

Wenelia only nodded in silence. For a moment, I feared these would be her only words – but then she spoke again, asking for some bread and water. Eventually, some colour returned to her cheeks and light to her eyes; she regained enough strength to ride a horse behind Ursula.

"It's too dangerous," I tell her. "This is Graelon's capital. He's the one who sent the Goths against your people. If his men find out who you are…"

She shrugs. "What more can they do to me? You saved my life, and that of my unborn child. That is a grave debt to repay."

"Why do you think you can help us?" asks Ursula. "Have you ever been to Worgium?"

"I have friends there. I know my way around it. I'll help you find whoever you're looking for."

I scratch my head and wince; I don't want to risk the life of someone we just fought so hard to rescue, but try as I might, I can't seem to be able to come up with a good reason to refuse her.

"Three is too many," I say. "Ursula, stay here. I'll go with Wenelia alone."

"And if the guards do recognise you?"

"They won't. I will go as Wenelia's Saxon slave. I look wretched enough for one. Nobody ever asks questions of a slave."

The Song of the Tides

CHAPTER IV
THE LAY OF EISHILD

Getting past the blockade proves easier than going anywhere near Graelon's *Praetorium*. The entrance to the *basilica* is heavily guarded, by both Briton and Goth warriors. More armed warriors stroll through the town in groups, patrolling the marketplace and the vicinity of the church.

"Why do we even need to get in there?" asks Wenelia.

"To contact Princess Ahes."

"That murderer's daughter?" She frowns. "What do you want with her?"

"She's the reason we're in Armorica. Trust me, she's not like the others. If I could at least send her a message… You said you had some friends here?"

She looks around. "We could try in that tavern," she says. "If you have coin."

"I took some silver from the Goths we slew… Are you sure they're *friends*?"

She scoffs and takes me to an ancient-looking establishment by the side of the market. It has no dining hall, only a long counter under a leaky roof, at which the patrons gather to drink and gossip. Wenelia takes a few pieces of Goth silver and leaves me there for a few minutes, before returning – alone, and with no silver.

The Song of the Tides

"Couldn't find anyone?" I ask.

"On the contrary. But they're not who you want to talk to. I asked them to find a way to send a message into the palace. If they can't do it, I doubt anyone can."

I stare at her in surprise. Just like Rhion, once she rested, she started carrying herself like a warrior. Even in her state, she exudes strength and power.

"Rhion and yourself – who are you, really?" I ask. "Not common villagers, that much is clear."

She draws me away from the tavern crowd and into a tight alleyway.

"We used to be just that, many years ago," she tells me when we're out of earshot of the guards. "Before the Britons came. Then they declared us all Bacauds, rebels, heathens – even though we were faithful Roman subjects for generations. When Patrician Budic tried to force us all out of our villages, Rhion and I rose against him. We held him at bay for a long time – until those *Capillati* came."

"The Goths."

She nods. "We never found out what they called themselves. Nor did we care. But they succeeded where the Britons failed – they pushed us into the woods and marshes, into the islands of the northern coast... It was Graelon who brought them to Armorica, I'm sure of it. He couldn't beat us, so he allied with some barbarians who did it for him – and now you tell me I should trust his spawn?"

"She's the only one who can help us – and explain what's really going on here."

"Fine. You'll have your messenger back before nightfall."

The messenger turns out to be a young girl, fair, tall and pale; a noble, judging by the fine dress and the amount of silver and gold she wears on her shoulders and around her neck – and not a Briton, judging by her long, golden hair.

"Are you… a Goth?" I ask. I grow anxious, sensing a trap, as does Wenelia at my side. Have we been betrayed by her tavern contacts?

"I am," the girl replies in good Latin. "But you needn't worry. *Fraujo* Ahes is my friend."

"What's your name?"

"Eishild. And I think I know what's yours. You must be Octa."

"She told you about me?"

The girl nods vigorously. She lowers her voice, even though there's nobody who could eavesdrop us here, in the cemetery on the outskirts of the town. "Is Marcus with you?"

I hesitate. How much can I really tell her?

"I'm not a spy," she insists.

"I need to know more before I can trust you."

The Song of the Tides

"The man you sent chose me to relay your message — shouldn't he be enough?"

"I don't know if I can trust him, either."

With an impatient sigh, Eishild reaches into her tunic and takes out a small piece of jewellery. I lift it to the light.

"What is it?" Wenelia asks.

"A Scots cloak brooch," I reply. "We fought them in Britannia. Ahes would show it to us to prove it's her… or someone who pretended to be her."

"I don't think you have much choice," says Eishild. "I am the only one who can get your words to the princess."

I look to Wenelia. She shrugs — her eyes tell me the predicament is my own to solve. She helped me use her contacts to find a messenger for the princess, and this is where her business in Worgium ends.

"Marcus is alive, and in Armorica," I say, at last. "But he's not here."

"I knew it. They told us you were all dead. But Ahes never believed them."

"We are very much alive — though I don't know for how long. You must tell the princess to meet us *tonight*. There's not a moment to spare."

"I'm sure she'll be eager to see you as soon as possible. Where should you meet?"

I pause again. It's obvious we have to meet outside of town — but not too far, if Ahes is to reach us before nightfall. I realise I don't know Worgium well enough to advise a good spot. There's only one place that both she and I would know how to find.

"Tell her — tell her to come to the place where Marcus and I spent the first night, three years ago."

"You still don't trust me." She nods. "Fine. I will pass on your message, and you will meet your princess tonight. You have my word."

"Octa! It really is you!"

She throws her arms around me, presses me to her chest and gives me a loud kiss on the forehead, before pulling away — and doing the same to Ursula.

"Then it is true? My beloved is alive?"

"Safe and sound when we last parted," I say. "Though he'll be growing hungry by now."

We intercept her on the road to her father's *villa* — just outside its gates. It's already dark; it took her longer to find us than I expected, and I was beginning to think our plan failed, and Eishild betrayed us after all, when she emerged from the night, accompanied only by one of her trusted servants, carrying a lamp of polished horn.

The Song of the Tides

"They said you all perished at sea," says Ahes, swallowing tears. "That the ship you were on crashed on the reefs off the northern coast."

"That much is true," I reply. "But we managed to land on some tiny island. Marcus and his men are still there, waiting for us to let them know what's going on here."

"What *is* going on?" asks Ursula. "We saw the Goths destroying villages on the way here. They said they were doing it on your father's orders. And what about the wedding?"

Ahes wipes her tears and grows serious. "The wedding is still on. But not to Marcus."

"Not to Marcus? Then to whom?"

"Hemnerith. Brother of the Goth king."

We fall silent. None of us imagined the full extent of Graelon's alliance with the Goths. Ursula is the first to express what we're both thinking, in a simple question:

"*Why?*"

Ahes sighs.

"It all started with that new *Magister Militum* in Gaul, Aegidius…"

"I know him," I say, remembering the man whose arrival four years ago in Cantia as Roman legate began my adventure in Gaul. Ahes looks up, surprised. "He's a decent man, and a good Roman," I say.

"Perhaps that's why my father couldn't agree with him… As soon as Aegidius secured his rule over Gaul, he began enforcing his law even here, in Armorica. He brought taxes and regulations upon the market at Redones, forbade us fighting Christians and banned trading them as slaves."

"That would've meant you Britons could no longer fight against the natives," I say. "Bacauds or not, the Armoricans are all Christians."

She nods. "At first, my father sent envoys to Trever with protests against the new rules, but they came back with nothing. Aegidius even threatened us with his Legions if we failed to obey his edicts. But what was even worse for my father and the other nobles were the new alliances Aegidius signed with Rome's neighbours."

"Hildrik and his Salians," I guess.

"The envoys returned with tales of the court at Trever filled with Frankish and Alan warriors. Heathens all, to a soul – and you know what that means to the likes of my father and Budic."

"Now I understand where the Goths came from," I say. "They, at least, are Christians."

"It was their King Theodrik who sent the offer of an alliance. He promised to deal with the Bacauds for my father – and with anyone who would stand in his way…"

"And to seal the alliance, you would have to marry his brother," says Ursula.

The Song of the Tides

Ahes hides her face in her hands. "I would never have agreed to this if I knew Marcus was still alive."

"This is why we were supposed to go down with that ship," I realise. "Graelon didn't want to anger Ambrosius by simply breaking the engagement – he wanted to keep the alliance with Britannia as well as with the Goths. An accident at sea would free his hand, and nobody would suspect any betrayal."

Ahes cries out in anguish. "I never thought my father would have been so cruel and duplicitous!"

Ursula gives me a knowing look. I bite my tongue not to express my surprise. Since our first meeting, I have seen Graelon for what he is: a smaller, weaker Wortimer; a selfish creature, interested only in the survival of himself and his closest kin. Getting rid of Marcus and his men, just to cement an alliance with the Goths that would enable him to slay countless more innocent villages, was exactly the kind of deceit I would've expected from him.

"What do the Goths get out of all this, I wonder?" asks Ursula.

"If they control Armorica, they can hold a knife to Aegidius's back," I reply. "They never gave up on conquering Gaul – the defeat at Arelate was only a setback. And if the rumours from Rome are true, the time to get their revenge may be nigh."

"Rumours from Rome?" asks Ahes.

"It could be nothing. A couple of months ago somebody told me they heard Maiorianus was dead."

"I heard this rumour, too," says Ahes, ashen faced. "From our Gothic 'allies'. But I dismissed it – how would these barbarians know what's happened to the Imperator?"

"The Goths are closer to Rome than anyone in Armorica or Britannia," I say. "In this one thing, I'd believe them." I rub my chin. "With the Imperator's death, all peace treaties with barbarian kingdoms are voided. If it's true, Gaul is in danger once again… How many warriors did this Hemnerith bring with him to Armorica?"

"I don't know. I'm not even sure my father knows. Could be hundreds, but they're scattered all over the province, hunting the Bacauds and burning the villages wherever they go – mostly in the east, along the border with Gaul."

"They're gathering plunder and forage for the coming war, no doubt. But…" I look to Ursula. "I don't know if there's anything *we* can do about it. Nor should we. We came here for a wedding, not to fight Goths."

"There will be no wedding as long as the Goths are here," says Ahes.

"That's not true," says Ursula. "You could just run away with us right now. Forget your father and his politics. Go back to Britannia, wed Marcus there, if that's what you really want."

"I… I thought about it when Eishild told me the news today," Ahes admits. "Yes, I could do it – I *want* to do it. An escape across the sea, a secret wedding… Like Paris and Helena in the Greek myths. But –" She lowers her gaze. "It's not just about me. I can't leave my people."

"Your people?" I ask. "What do they have to do with it?"

"Not everyone agrees with my father's alliance with the Goths," Ahes explains. "The men who fought with me in Britannia, the ships' crews – they are loyal subjects of the *Comes*, for now, but they are ready to rise in anger, if only someone gives them the word."

"You would be crushed without mercy," I say. "The Goths are second only to the Huns in their reputation for war and cruelty."

"This is why we haven't done anything yet. But now that Marcus is here –"

"Marcus is *not* here," I remind her. "Though I wish he was. Maybe he'd manage to talk some sense into you. You can't possibly hope to fight the Goths."

"Warus and his ship are in port at Gesocribate," says Ahes. "If you tell him where that island is, he'll bring them all back in no time."

"Well then, what are we waiting for?" I stand up. "Wake up the others – we ride to Gesocribate!"

Two days later, I watch the *Maegwind* drop anchor – not in the Gesocribate harbour itself, but deeper in the bay, hidden from view by a small islet linked to the mainland by a narrow tidal causeway. A small boat sets out from the islet; it takes agonisingly long for it to ferry the Dumnonians over. Marcus arrives last, to make sure everyone got safely across. Ahes doesn't wait for him to step out of the boat; she leaps on him with a squeal. Her lips join his in a long, passionate kiss.

"Here," I say, handing the *Decurion* a sack filled with bread and sausages. "You must be starving."

I notice that the small boat sets off on one more journey. "What's this?" I ask.

"The crew of the ship – and Rhion's companions. I managed to convince some of them to join us."

"*Join* you? Do they know what's going on here?"

"Only that their princess is marrying a Goth instead of a Briton. It's enough to rile them to anger."

I glance at Ursula. "I wonder how many more of Graelon's subjects are quietly discontent with their king's decision. Maybe we could use that."

"We don't have much time to find out," she replies. "The wedding is in a couple of weeks."

"We'll figure something out – as soon as my men are fed and rested," Marcus says.

He looks around. The isle was once part of Gesocribate harbour itself, and before that, it was itself a fortress, the memory of which is retained in the name: *Cair Inis*, Isle of the Fort. A ring of earthen wall still surrounds the shore, bounding within it ruins of the Roman village – a few streets with traces of stone wharfs and shops, and a square space that once would have been a market, all now grown over with ferns and shrubs. Nobody lives here anymore – the Britons, having removed what remained of the previous inhabitants, themselves preferred to move to the mainland, near the ancient *garum* vats – and so the isle was the perfect place to conceal Marcus's arrival.

"One could defend this place for months," he notes approvingly.

"Not when the tide is out," says Ahes. "You'll see later."

While Warus's ship moves past the isle to finally moor in the harbour, we watch as the receding tide uncovers first the narrow causeway, then a land bridge of sand and rock. Soon, some children appear on the pebbles, searching for crabs and shrimps trapped in the shallow pools, followed by adults picking mussels from the exposed rock face.

"We have to wait until sundown," says Ahes.

"That should be enough time to come up with a plan to stop your father and his Goth allies," says Marcus. "Are you with me, Octa?"

"If you can convince me, we have a chance."

"We'll see about that." He turns to Ahes. "First of all, my love, tell me where I can get some good horses for my men?"

"One thing's certain – there aren't enough of us to challenge the Goths on our own, even if it is just a small warband," I say after everyone gathers on what was once Cair Inis town square, around a large bonfire. At night, we don't need to conceal our presence: according to Ahes, the youths of

Gesocribate often cross the causeway to seek romantic seclusion in the ruins, so nobody will be surprised by a fire being lit among the crumbling walls.

"We've enough to overrun Worgium," says Ursula. "There can't be more than a few dozen *vigiles* in that town."

"Hemnerith's household guard, the *Gardingi*, is stationed in Worgium," says Ahes. "Twenty warriors, veterans of wars in Hispania, where they also fought a Bacaud rebellion on Rome's behalf. And if he's threatened, more will come from the countryside."

Any hope I had for Marcus to be the cool-headed one and convince Ahes of the folly of her plan to fight the Goths were dashed as soon as he arrived and heard her story. He made an immediate choice: to defeat the Gothic chieftain, Hemnerith, and somehow force his men out of Armorica, not just to save the *Decurion*'s wedlock, but to thwart any new designs the Goth army might have against Gaul and Rome.

"Shouldn't we let Aegidius know about this first?" I asked him. "His forces would be much better equipped to deal with a threat this size."

"Even if we had enough time, I'm sure the Goths would intercept any messengers we'd send across the border. Besides, we have surprise on our side. They'll never expect us. With your help, Octa, I'm sure we can win this. You're the hero of Trever and *Cair* Wortigern – what is a handful of Goths to you?"

"We have to draw them out," I say now, resigned to the fight. Marcus and Ahes are my friends; I can't just leave them to battle the Goths by themselves. And he's right – though whatever force Hemnerith brought here would be insignificant compared to the vast armies the Gothic king commands in his southern lands, defeating them would no doubt help *Magister* Aegidius protect his domain from the barbarian threat – and show him once again how valuable Iute warriors are as his allies.

My father would've done the same.

"Scatter the Goths in the woods," I continue. "Spread as much chaos throughout Armorica as we can. We are few, but we are fast riders – we have to fight like forest bandits: strike at camps, destroy patrols, disrupt forage. I did this at Trever, and my father fought Wortimer in Londin in the same manner. It's the only way."

"My people will join you," says Wenelia from across the bonfire. "If I can get the message to them."

"You're not going anywhere in your state," I oppose. "We'll find some other way."

"The Goths didn't mind my state when they killed my man and tortured me," she replies bitterly. "I am not yet so far gone that I can't be of use. Give me a horse and two men of guard, and I will set this countryside on fire."

"If the Bacauds join our side, all the Britons will stand against us," says Marcus. "Even those opposing Ahes's wedlock."

"We'll have to keep them separated," I agree. "Your people will have to keep to their villages, Wenelia. Otherwise the city dwellers will think you're rising against *them*, not the Goths."

Marcus nods in agreement. "I was thinking the same. But without the Bacauds, we would still need some sizeable force to reach Hemnerith."

"Not if we lay an ambush," says Audulf.

He's been keeping quiet throughout our council – he's never been to Armorica before, and hasn't met Marcus or Ahes; he's not familiar with the complicated situation in the province other than what I briefly explained to him and the rest of the Iutes on our arrival; but he's as good a warrior as any of us and, after Ursula, my closest friend, so I'm always ready to hear his opinion.

"It goes without saying," says Marcus. "But this is a land of low hills and sparse woods. There aren't many good places for an ambush this size."

Audulf shrugs. "I don't know this place as well as you do, but I'm sure we can figure something out. There's always a way."

Marcus yawns and puts his arm around Ahes. "We can return to this when we put in motion the first step of our plan," he says. "I don't think there's anything more that we need to come up with tonight."

"Very well." I stand up and brush the dust of a crumbled town from my bottom. "Don't forget we have to cross the causeway before dawn."

"The tide's about to come back in," says Ahes. "We won't be able to cross for a few hours."

"Enough to get some sleep," says Ursula. She pulls on my tunic sleeve and drags me away from the bonfire. "Let's leave them alone," she tells me quietly. "You can see they'd rather spend this time with each other than discuss war plans."

We stroll to the edge of the isle and sit on top of the earthen bank. The lights of Gesocribate shimmer across the causeway as the town prepares for the night. Though it's now far from any land route, the port must have once been a target for pirate raids, for it is bound by a stone wall facing the sea. The rampart cuts off the harbour and the beach from the rest of the town, with only a single gate facing the quay and the causeway. The guards set ablaze braziers on the two corner towers. On a hill above town, somebody lights the tower beacon, guiding stray vessels towards the harbour. Fishermen drag their boats out onto the pebble beach. The ropes on Graelon's ships twang in the wind.

Ursula lays her head on my shoulder.

"We should've got wedded before we came here," she says.

"I thought we already were."

"The proper way. In Dorowern. With our parents' blessing."

"You haven't spoken of it for three years. Why the sudden change of heart?"

She nods back towards the campfire, where we left Marcus and Ahes. "It's their fault," she says. "They made me think about what could happen. How Fate could force us apart."

"It wasn't Fate that pulled Ahes and Marcus apart, but her father," I say.

"It was Fate that forced Graelon to seek allies beyond Britannia. What if my mother decides to marry me off to some Londin noble, to raise the family prestige? What if *Rex* Aeric sends you to wed some Frankish princess to strengthen the alliance with Hildrik? It's one thing if one of us dies in battle somewhere, I accept that, it's all part of being a warrior – but for both of us to be alive and forever separated? I don't know what I would do…"

"My father would never do something like that against my will."

"You can't know that for certain."

I stare at the quiet, dark sea in silence. Ursula and I rarely discuss our feelings. I can't even remember if we ever confessed our love for one another; surely, we must have at some point in the last three years, drunk on mead at one of my father's feasts?

"They're very at ease with each other, aren't they?" I say.

"And why shouldn't they be?" asks Ursula.

"I… I don't know. Why aren't we like that?"

She shrugs. "We're not like any other couple I know. Because we're not like any other *people* I know."

The Song of the Tides

"*You* certainly aren't…" I hold her tighter and kiss her brow gently.

Two youths run out of the shrubs, half-naked. They dash past us – taking us for just another couple enjoying the island's isolation – and leap down from the shore onto the causeway.

The reason for their haste soon becomes apparent. Starting with a rustle and a ripple, the sea assaults the causeway from both sides in a violent rush. I have lived most of my life on the coast, and I have seen countless tides flow and ebb, but I have never witnessed one as fierce as this one; it's as if the sea broke through a dyke. By the time the fleeing couple reaches the other side of the strait, they have to wade in knee-deep water, coming at them in rolling, foam-topped waves.

I leap up, struck by a sudden idea.

"What is it?" Ursula asks, startled.

"I know what we need to do."

Ubba's head appears in the hut's door.

"She's here."

"Let her in," I say with a wave.

The girl enters, throws down her travelling hood and blinks a few times as her eyes grow used to the lamp's light. The night outside is pitch-black, the moon hidden behind a thick cover of clouds. The abandoned farm where we meet lies a little over a mile south of Worgium; it must have been a difficult journey in the dark, across damp fields cut through by cold brooks and tall hedges, even with Ubba and Croha as guides.

I invite Eishild to sit down. She hesitates, looking at the flea-ridden mat at her feet. The hut is otherwise empty — there's barely a roof over our heads; the unfortunate Armorican family, to which the farm once belonged, have been banished or slain by Graelon's warriors, and all their possessions were plundered or destroyed.

The girl puts her cloak over the mat before sitting. The little gesture tells me that my suspicions about her were right.

"Before I include you in our plans," I say, "I need to know who you really are, and why you would join us against your own kin."

She glances to Ursula, sitting at my side. Her presence makes the girl calmer; she exhales and straightens her back.

"I am Eishild," she begins. "Daughter of Thaurismod, the rightful *Rix* of the Goths."

Her eyes gleam with pride — then, with disappointment. She expects the revelation to strike us like lightning; but what she doesn't know is that I, myself, am an heir to a *Rex*, and in my short life, so far, I have counted kings, queens and *Duces* as my friends. Meeting yet another barbarian princess does not impress me as much as she imagines it might.

"Explain," I say. "Who is this Thaurismod, and why is he no longer your king?"

The Song of the Tides

"How much do you know about us, Goths?" she asks.

"I know you came from the East, already Christians," I reply. "That you sacked Rome, but then allied with the Empire and were allowed to settle in Gaul. That you fought the Huns at Maurica, and were betrayed by Aetius, and have had no reason to trust Rome ever since."

She's impressed by my knowledge – I can tell she did not expect it from a barbarian from some remote northern island beyond the borders of the Empire. But my father often used the example of how the Goths were treated at Maurica to justify his mistrust of Rome – and I knew at least one man who fought in the great battle himself: Odo, the Gaulish *Decurion* who taught me everything I know about cavalry warfare.

"My father was the eldest son of the first Theodrik, the victor at Maurica," Eishild replies. "But because of Rome's betrayal, he lost the respect of his courtiers. Two years after defeating the Huns, he was slain by assassins sent by my step-uncles. Hemnerith was one of them."

I nod, tapping my thumb on the chin. The story is a familiar one: a member of a powerful family kills another to take his place. It is how Hildrik took the throne of the Salians – and how, according to my father, Aelle took power over the Saxons. What is rare, however, is that there should remain any relatives of the deceased ruler…

"Why did they let you live?" Ursula asks, thinking the same as me.

"Because they are not heathens," Eishild replies, oddly proud of her murderous uncles.

"Their faith didn't stop them from spilling your father's blood," I note. "It's more likely that they're planning to use you in some way in the future. What happened after Thaurismod's death? Was the tribe united behind the new king?"

"Yes, I suppose you're right…" She slumps. "We *are* a divided people – and were even before my father's murder. The split strikes even through our family."

"What is it? A feud between clans?"

"Worse – it's our religion."

"There are still heathens among Goths?" I raise my eyebrow. "After all this time?"

"It would be easier if there were," Eishild scoffs. "No, we have all been Christians since my great-grandfather's days. We are proud to have been the first baptised among all fair-hairs. But it was so long ago that even Rome has moved on since then. The Goths, through their refusal to embrace the change, are now regarded as heretics by the Bishops and Imperators of Rome… At least those who keep to the old ways."

"And which ways do you follow?" I ask. I don't want to know any more details about the division; the intricacies of the Christian heresies have evaded me, even when Bishop Fastidius tried to explain them. The Bishops of Rome have always been too keen to call anyone heretic who disagreed with their specific variation of Christian faith: Pelagius, the Scillonian priests, and now the Goths… But if there truly is a division running deep throughout Theodrik's kingdom, it would be foolish not to exploit it.

The Song of the Tides

"My grandmother was a Gaul, and she taught my father the Roman creed," she replies. "When she died, my grandfather wedded a Gothic princess, and the sons she gave him all followed the old faith."

"I think I see now," says Ursula. "Your uncles fear that if they killed you, too, the new Christians among the Goths would rise against them."

Eishild falls silent, as if only now realising her own importance. She plucks at the threads in the mat in thought.

"This explains why you live – but not why you're *here*," I say. "What's the point of dragging you all the way from Tolosa to this rain-drenched arsehole of a place?"

"My uncles want me to marry one of Graelon's courtiers," she replies. "To further strengthen the alliance. And since I'm the only one who worships in the same way as these Britons…" She shrugs, resigned to her fate.

"Are you to be wedded on the same day as Hemnerith and Ahes?" asks Ursula.

"I think so – if I agree to it… I haven't even met my betrothed yet. I think his name is… Budic?"

"Patrician Budic?" I exclaim. "I thought he already had a wife."

"I believe she died a year ago – if we're talking about the same man."

I look to Ursula. "It's almost too fortunate," I say in Iutish.

[98]

"Whether it's fortune or Fate, we must embrace it," she replies. "The question is: do we trust this girl to do what we ask of her?"

I turn back to Eishild. "Many Goth warriors will perish in this fight who have nothing to do with your father's murder," I say.

She looks up with a fierce gleam in her eyes.

"Those twenty who came here with Hemnerith, the *Gardingi*, were all involved in Theodrik's takeover of the kingdom. They all come from my stepmother's clan. There are no innocents among them."

"And you'd help us, even if it means weakening your people?"

"Theodrik has thousands of warriors under his command. He won't even notice these few gone." She shrugs. "In a way, I'll be helping him, and the tribe. Sooner or later the surviving brothers will fight each other for succession, and it will be a shorter conflict if I help eliminate one of them here."

I wave my hand. "I'm not here to learn of the inner goings-on of the Gothic kingdom. I've heard enough to trust that you'll be willing to help us."

"Just let me know what I need to do," she says. She clenches her fists on the edge of her cloak with determination.

"First of all," I start, "you need to agree to that wedlock with Patrician Budic. Make sure it's on the same day as Hemnerith's – we'll let you know the date… But you present them with one, crucial condition."

The Song of the Tides

CHAPTER V
THE LAY OF AHES

The riders in the vanguard of the Gothic column glance around nervously. Their hands rest on the hilts of their swords. They peer through the foliage, trying to penetrate the gloom under the boughs with their gaze. Each rustle in the leaves, each bough broken under the foot of a startled animal makes them stop and investigate the disturbance. They are right to be anxious. The column marches down the finest ambush place in all of Armorica: a twenty-mile long, deep ravine, as straight as a Roman road, cutting through the hills south of Worgium. The sides of the ravine rise a hundred feet over the floor, steep and overgrown with dense, dark forest. And just as the Goths suspect, my men are set up on top of both of those sides.

None of them are warriors – or at least, they weren't until about a week ago. Contrary to what the Britons imagined, the natives were not all "Bacauds"; most of the Martinian bandits threatening Armorican *villas* were wiped out early in the Goth campaign, and what was left were just simple village folk, driven into the woods and marshes from their razed villages. It took Wenelia a long time to find enough of them willing to join our fight and form into something resembling a warband.

All that is left of that warband after days of marching and fighting their way across Armorica, is now with me in the ravine. We lost more than a half of what we started out with – I had no time to turn these poor people into fighters, so all we could count on in battle was their tenacity, numbers – and surprise. The Britons and the Goths are recent guests to this land; the Armoricans know its every corner. Just as Audulf predicted, they knew all the best places for ambushes and traps, even in this flat, featureless land. They were the ones who told me of this ravine, and how we could lure the Gothic column into it by flooding a nearby stream and blocking the main road to Worgium.

I adjust the mail coat I took from the fallen Goth chief – an Armorican blacksmith did his best to make it fit me, but he lacked the necessary skill and metal to ensure it didn't chafe around the neck and arms. I lay my hand on Croha's shoulder and give her a squeeze. It's only the two of us here out of my band of Iutes. Somewhere else in Armorica, Ursula and Audulf each lead two other groups of villagers on similar missions; Marcus and his *equites* are somewhere out there, too, fighting alongside a small group of Britons loyal to Ahes, performing their lightning strikes along the Roman highways and river crossings. It is as Wenelia had promised: the entire countryside of Armorica is on fire, and the Goths, so haughty and bold at first, have quickly learned to fear the dark woods and the steep hills. To deal with the growing threat, Hemnerith had no choice but to send out more and more of his warriors against us, until all that was left in the camps around Worgium were his twenty *Gardingi* – and this one last column, marching before us, heading back to the town from a patrol on the southern coast.

The forward guard passes the narrowest point in the ravine; they ride out onto a broad, fan-shaped plain spreading out at the mouth of the valley. The road to Worgium passes through here, and it's less than ten miles to the town, over the open plain; I can sense the riders' relief when they see it. They halt on the side of the road, waiting for the column of footmen to catch up to them.

I put the war horn to my lips and blow the charge. Croha leaps forward, followed by the rest of the Armoricans. They try their best to form a wedge behind her, but most of them just tumble down the slope, waving their simple weapons and screaming curses at the Goths below.

We smash at the column from both sides, like the waves of a surging tide on the Caer Inis causeway. Propelled by the impact of the downhill charge, I thrust my sword into the back of the first enemy that appears before me; the weapon goes right through his mail coat and goes out the other way. I kick him off the blade, wipe it on my tunic and search for a new target. All around me is chaos; the Armoricans, filled with vengeful wrath, hack with their hatchets, slash with their sickles and strike with their clubs at every Goth they can reach. Limbs fly, blood spurts in rivers, groans of pain and gurgling cries of agony fill the air. I spot the enemy chief, at the front, desperately trying to bring order to the line of his troops. He, too, holds a war horn at his lips, of twisted bronze, shaped like a dragon's head. In response to his call, the three vanguard riders turn back. I reach down and grab a spear from the hands of a Goth warrior, clubbed to death by three Armorican villagers.

"Croha! With me!" I call. I grab two more men and we rush to the front of the column. I point out one of the riders to Croha. She nods and draws the two flying axes from her belt. I charge at the other with my spear and order the two Armoricans to attack the third.

Croha's first axe hits the horse's flanks – and bounces off the thick blanket that protects the beast's hide. But the second flies true and strikes the rider on the shoulder with enough force to throw him off his mount. I have no time to admire Croha's feat; the second rider rushes at me with his lance. I dodge it and thrust the spear into the belly of his horse. With a push and a twist, I tear a great gash in the poor animal's stomach, until all the guts fall out and the beast falls on its side, crushing the rider underneath.

The third rider, who by now has managed to slay one of the villagers assaulting him, sees what happened to his comrades and, despite furious shouts from his chief, turns tail and flees. I look to Croha, but she just shrugs, helplessly – without her axes, she can't do anything to stop the runaway. Besides, we are soon overwhelmed by the rest of the Goths, storming our way, desperate to get out of the murderous ravine.

I pick up the sword again and face the wave of panicked enemy. I hack and slash through mail and cloth, not stopping to see what effect my blows have on the Goths; every time I sense the blade squelch into flesh, I count it as a kill. Behind me, a line of Armoricans closes off the exit from the valley, picking off all that go past me. Pushing through the crowd, I reach the chief; he doesn't spot me until it's too late. He spins, trying to avoid my falling blade, and parries my sword with his, but his block is clumsy; the weapon slips from his bloodied hand, and I sink my sword into his shoulder. Another stream of fleeing Goths separates us; when I see him again, he's far away, climbing up the northern slope, abandoning his people to the bloodbath below.

I whistle at Croha. Together, we climb out of the ravine onto the fan-shaped plain. I look back at the slaughter; it's impossible to count how many men we've lost, or how many Goths' lives we have taken. The surviving Armoricans want to chase after the few enemy warriors that got away, but I stop them; there's no point wasting strength on fruitless pursuit. We're too close to Worgium – any moment now

Hemnerith will launch a relief force, which is bound to destroy us. We have to vanish into the woods before this happens.

Another rider appears on the road, coming from Worgium, alone. I order the men to scatter out of sight. Croha and I hide in a bush on the side of the road, until I see who it is: young Drustan, one of Marcus's *equites*.

"It is time," he says. "Hemnerith agreed to move the wedding to the date Eishild proposed."

"Good," I say, wiping sweat and blood from my brow with a weary gesture. "That means we finally riled him into action. Are all the preparations proceeding as planned?"

"As far as I know, yes."

A Goth warrior at my feet groans and stirs awake. Without looking, I thrust my sword through his chest.

"Very well," I say, cleaning the blade with my tunic. "Tell your *Decurion* everything will be ready for his arrival at Gesocribate."

I wonder how much this must have cost Graelon, and how long it took his weavers to prepare it: a carpet of flower petals, red and white, over a thousand feet long, scattered across the entire causeway from the Gesocribate quay to the shore of Cair Inis. And all of it to be used just for this one occasion, for only one purpose: so that the feet of Hemnerith, Ahes, their guests and their guards are not muddied with the dirt of the exposed sea floor.

The Song of the Tides

Hemnerith's *Gardingi* are the first to step onto the flowery carpet, ten warriors in front of him, ten warriors behind. Each of them looks like a clan chief himself. They all have their long, luscious golden hair bound with diadems of silver and jewels; they don tunics studded with steel scales thrown over their mail coats; they wear golden *torcs* around their necks and silver and bronze bands around their arms.

Hemnerith, marching in the middle, wears the finest jewels and the brightest armour. He alone wears a helmet: it is the headgear of a Roman officer, with a red feathered crest, adorned with gold plate and studded with silver nails. The rubies and sapphires inlaid into the hilt of his sword gleam in the sun. He stops in the middle of the causeway and turns around to take in the view of the bay, the shimmering sea and the harbour walls, resplendent with garlands of flowers and draperies of precious cloth.

Eishild and Ahes had little trouble convincing him to hold the wedding ceremony on the island, instead of Gesocribate itself. With the Bacaud uprising still raging throughout the countryside, and the fighting coming close even to the walls of Worgium, the Goth chieftain appreciated the safety afforded by the isolated island. He didn't care for the wedding being witnessed by the Briton townsfolk; no doubt, he planned to throw a feast for his own people when he returned with Ahes to Tolosa. This, here, was only a ritual, a simple ceremony, little more than signing a treaty of alliance with Graelon and his nobles. Even better if it could all be done in a secure, secluded place, away from any threat of the rebels and prying eyes of Aegidius's spies.

I'm still not sure what it is that the Goths are gaining through this double wedding. The cold, fallow, mist-shrouded wastes of Armorica are worthless compared to the riches of

Hispania and Septimania, where *Rix* Theodrik prefers to focus the attention of his warriors. The only prize here worth taking is the possibility of flanking Aegidius from the west, should Theodrik decide to march against Gaul, but is this enough reason to give his brother away to an Armorican princess – and his niece to some lesser noble?

The second party to cross the causeway after the Goths are the Britons: Graelon and Budic, with a small retinue of noble families. I can't see Graelon's face, but I imagine it's sour. He certainly *did* want a great wedding feast, filled with guests, gawped on by countless admiring onlookers. He wanted the prestige of this wedding to spill out all over Armorica, for it to be written about in chronicles and spoken about in taverns from Worgium to Redones. An alliance with the great Gothic kingdom is going to make him as powerful as his hated rival Ambrosius. Perhaps it would even make him one day strong enough to go back to Britannia and conquer the squabbling nobles.

But he is the junior partner in this enterprise, and must obey Hemnerith's whims. If Hemnerith declares the wedding is to take place on a small island, then it must be so. And if Hemnerith demands that, for his and his people's safety, the entire area around the harbour has to be cleared of anyone who could be deemed suspicious, then all the townsfolk of Gesocribate must be exiled from their homes for a day and watch the ceremony from the distance of the surrounding hills. Even the ships were forced to sail away from the quays and throw anchor in the bay. There isn't a soul left in the town or on the island, except the servants preparing the ceremony, the soldiers guarding it – and the slaves.

I am one of those slaves, clad only in a torn, drab tunic and loincloth, pulling a two-wheeled cart loaded with the

The Song of the Tides

furnishing for the wedding: stools and benches for the noble guests, animal hides and straw mats for the others; the flower carpet is too precious to have it trampled with horse hooves, so the vehicles must be drawn by men. Behind us, the last of the carts carries victuals for the brief feast that is to take place after the wedding ceremony. Before us, carried in a litter, ride the two brides, Ahes and Eishild, and the local priest who will oversee the ceremony, Father Constantin. Graelon would've preferred the bishop from Redones, but no amount of gold and jewels could've convinced him to travel across a country burning with open rebellion.

Thanks to the loyalty of the men in Ahes's service, most of the "slaves" are part of the conspiracy. Audulf, Eolh and Deor are hiding among the cart pullers; Ubba and Croha concealed themselves under the blankets and cloth on the wagons; Hleo and Haering, disguised as fishermen – not a difficult feat for them – observe the procession from their boat, bobbing on the water on the northern side of the bay. Only Ursula's not here: her presence would've been too conspicuous. She's with Marcus and his *equites* in their hiding place, waiting for their turn.

We heave the cart up the tall shore and onto the island. The guards point us to a space cleared from rubble and scrubs, where we are to unload the goods and set up the feast. I try to glance towards the market square, where the ceremony is to take place, but a guard thumbs me over the head.

"Watch where you're going, barbarian slave," he snarls. "Don't sully our princess with your filthy gaze."

"Yes, master," I reply, bowing. I pick up a heavy folding stool. "Where should I put this?"

"How should I know?" He shrugs. "Set up the windbreaks first, or the breeze will make everything damp."

"Of course — how wise."

As soon as we finish setting up the feast, a fanfare of trumpets announces the start of the ceremony at the town square. The guards are no longer interested in us, as long as we stay out of the way of the nobles. We take up the carts again and drag them back onto the causeway, where I have them set up in a line, with only a narrow gap in the middle.

I whistle a signal. The hiding warriors climb out of the wagons. Each of us carrying an *amphora* filled with lamp oil, we sneak along the shore to the far end of the isle, where last night we gathered bundles of dry straw and firewood, and hid buckets of pitch.

While my men scatter the straw mixed with pitch around the ruins, and pour oil on it, I find a gap in the wall, covered with dense gorse, through which I have a good view of the wedding; looking the other way, I can see the ships gathered in the outer bay. Warus's *Maegwind* was allowed to stand the closest to the island, as a sign of respect to Ahes's mother; it flies the banner of Graelon — the black triple knot on white cloth — and Hemnerith's red raven underneath it.

As it is a wedding among Christians, and it's a Sunday, it is preceded by a Holy Mass, conducted by Father Constantin over a field altar made from a flat slab of stone laid upon the remains of a pillar. The priest, brought at the last moment, is clearly overwhelmed by the occasion: he stumbles reading the Scripture, stutters on the blessings and almost drops the holy bread. Graelon glowers at him throughout the rite, while Hemnerith appears amused, whispering jests to his companions, to which they respond with badly hidden sniggers. At length, Graelon grows impatient, and anxious. He grunts at the priest to hurry.

Father Constantin hastily recites the final prayer, blesses the gathered one last time and requests the first betrothed couple to step before him. The trumpets sound again. The acolytes swiftly remove the trappings of the mass and put them away in a silver-bound chest. Not waiting for them to finish, Budic steps brusquely up to the altar and nods at Hemnerith. The Goth approaches, presenting Eishild as the bride. Like Ahes, waiting in line behind her, she's wearing a wreath of flowers on her head, and a long robe of roughly woven cloth. The veil hides the grimace of disgust on her face as she and Budic join their hands and the priest binds them with sacred cloth. It appears this is to be at once a betrothal and a wedding, which makes me wonder just how recently the idea of this alliance occurred to Graelon and Theodrik.

I glance towards the mainland. Right about now, if everything went according to plan, Marcus and his men should be climbing the ramparts of Gesocribate, getting rid of the guards and taking over the towers and the gates. I can't see if they've been successful from here, but I have no doubt in their capabilities. I've seen them capture the walls of the fortress of Segont; the Armorican town is easy prey to these skilled hunters.

Father Constantin lifts his hands in a blessing and raises his eyes to the sky; it is a clear, blue day, with barely a cloud in sight, but there's a stiff breeze from the sea, bending the boughs, rustling the leaves and tearing at the rich robes of the gathered. The priest recites a brief prayer, then lays a kiss on the brows of Eishild and Budic. The Briton groom turns back to the gathered and raises his hand in triumph. The Goths erupt in loud cheers – not for Budic, not even for Eishild; they simply appear to be enjoying the wedding itself. As Budic unveils Eishild's face to kiss her, Hemnerith's companions produce clay mugs they had earlier filled with ale, and smash them against the stone floor. The uproar helps Eishild hide her wince of disgust as Budic slobbers over her youthful lips.

The two of them make way for the main event: the joining of Ahes and Hemnerith. Just as the couple step up to the altar, Ubba taps me on the shoulder and points towards the sea.

"*Aetheling*, look!"

I turn to see the *Maegwind* drop its mainsail. The cloth unfurls in the breeze, revealing the embroidered figure of Ahes's mother.

"Is this the signal?" asks Ubba.

"Yes," I say. It was Warus who, based on his long experience of sailing these waters, told us what the best date for the wedding would be; but even he could not foretell the exact hour for the attack without observing the sea with his own eyes, on the day. "Go tell the others. Hurry."

He rushes off with the orders. I reach for the war horn, hidden under my cloak. It's not yet the time to use it. First, my Iutes must set fire to the oil-soaked bundles. I'm not sure if the stratagem will work here as well as it did in Hrodha's fort on Mona; the air is damp with the sea breeze, the area to cover is greater, and Hemnerith's warriors are more experienced in handling ambushes by the rebels… But there

The Song of the Tides

is one thing that I'm counting on them not knowing: the fickle and violent tides of the Great Sea.

From what I've read, and what Eishild told us, the Goths had arrived in the West from the great seas of grass and deep forests that lay to the east of the Empire. The only waters they knew there were lakes and rivers. And while they dwelled for a time on the shores of the *Mediterraneum* on the way here, that inland sea was always calm and unmoving. Only a few years ago did Theodrik's warriors reach the shores of Aquitania and Armorica; the Great Sea is still a mysterious creature to them.

As Father Constantin begins the final part of the ceremony – the blessing of Ahes's and Hemnerith's union – the flames burst all around the island. Small and scattered at first, then, as my Iutes throw more fuel onto the fire, and roll the flaming bales towards the centre of the island, a circle of conflagration surrounds the town square on three sides – with the exception of the causeway.

Hemnerith reaches for his sword – but his weapon lies with the others in a pile at the entrance to the square, which, for the duration of the ceremony, is sacred ground. His warriors rush to get them. I raise the horn and blow the signal. The Iutes, the Bacauds and the loyal Armoricans leap out of their hiding places. We emerge onto the square with the fires blazing behind our backs; my warriors, their faces smudged black with soot, screaming and wildly waving weapons and torches, appear like monsters from Hell. The Britons, stunned by our audacity, are easy prey; I cut down one of the guards, and thrust the sword through another within seconds, though I try not to harm any of the nobles, knowing some of them are Ahes's family. The Goths, however, soon shake off their surprise; but even they can't gather into a defensive line swiftly enough in the narrow confines of the town's ruins. Before long, the first of the *Gardingi* falls under the blows of my men.

The servants are the first to break and flee – but Graelon's soldiers and Hemnerith's warriors stand fast in the face of our onslaught, as I'd guessed they would. In the chaos, my eyes meet those of Ahes. I nod. The girl shrieks in panic, tears her hand out of Hemnerith's grasp and runs away towards the causeway.

Eishild picks up a shield from the pile of weapons, but instead of standing in the line beside her kin, she also retreats, calling to her men in their language; Hemnerith turns to her, furious. For a few moments, they argue, shouting at each other over the length of the square, until another of his Goths falls dead, with Croha's axe in his chest. This, it seems, is too much for the Goth warchief.

"Back!" Hemnerith calls to his men and the Britons. "To the causeway!"

Graelon protests; he knows what can happen to those who stay too long on the treacherous strip of rock. But Hemnerith trusts his skill and experience of his warriors more than he does the Briton's urgings. For him, it makes far better sense to make a stand on the narrow causeway, rather than fight the ambush on all sides.

The Goths pull away from our attack, in an orderly column. Graelon and Budic gather their men to form a rear guard. The Britons remain reluctant to follow after Hemnerith, but abandoned by their allies, they have little choice and they, too, push back towards the strait.

The Song of the Tides

I split my troop in half, leave one half to harass Graelon's Britons while the rest of us makes our way again around the isle's shore, back to where we left the wagons. We reach it just in time – the Goths have just pushed through the gap between the carts and are now wading across the causeway. The sea is already rising around them, but, at first, they fail to notice the slow trickle. When they reach halfway across, Marcus, his *equites* and a few dozen loyal townsfolk appear on the opposite shore, and line up along the quayside with shields and spears at the ready. The town gates are shut behind them. Hemnerith must now make his decision. Climbing out against Marcus's blades is going to be a hard slog; he looks back and sees my men, pulling the wagons together to block his way back onto the island and stop Graelon from coming to his aid. He is trapped.

The flames on the isle die down, dampened by the breeze. I hear the fighting closing in beyond the wagons, but I can't spare any of my warriors to aid those standing against the Britons. I have all my Iutes with me, at least, and it is their survival that I must look to. To the north, I glance Hleo and Haering leading a small flotilla of fishing boats as the third prong of the attack towards the quickly sinking causeway. They make ready their darts and javelins, to throw as soon as they're within range.

Hemnerith – holding Ahes in a tight grip by his side – orders his warriors to form a tight circle around him. The water now reaches up to their knees and laps at their thighs. I can almost taste their growing fear. Riders of the great eastern plains, like the Huns, these Goths have a natural dread of the ocean, on the shores of which generations of Iutes, Britons and Armoricans have spent our entire lives. They could try to break through the wagons, back onto the island – it would be easier to return, with the Briton nobles attacking us from the other side, than pushing against Marcus's trained soldiers, up the steep shore. But that would mean staying on the isle at the mercy of the tide; the Goths don't know how deep the sea here can get. What if it swallows the isle whole?

"Hemnerith!" Marcus booms over the churning waves, shaking his sword. "Face *me* if you have the courage!"

The Goth warchief laughs. "Are you Marcus of Dumnonia?" he asks. "I've heard of you. I thought you were dead! No matter, you will not be alive for long."

He draws his sword, but in this, he momentarily lets go of Ahes. The girl rushes towards Marcus. Hemnerith reaches out, grabs her by the hair and pulls her back to him.

"Let go of her, you coward!" shouts Marcus.

"I will – once you let me on shore, so we can have a fair fight!" the Goth shouts back.

The sea now reaches to his thighs, and he's finding it difficult to stand among the billows. He orders his warriors to wade towards the land. Behind me, I hear Graelon's men push and hack at the wagons; my Iutes push back against them, but I can see they will not hold out for long.

"Don't listen to him, my love!" Ahes cries, but Marcus's resolve wavers. Without the advantage of high ground, his *equites* will be crushed by Hemnerith's heavily armoured veterans – and everything we fought for will be for naught. I know better than anyone what is going on in his heart right now. I spot Ursula on the far end of the *Decurion's* line, staring at what unravels with a pained expression. Why must men always resolve their quarrels by threatening women?

The Song of the Tides

Before either of the men can do anything else, Eishild cries out and throws herself on Hemnerith. As I watch what happens next, it is as if the world around me has slowed down. I see Eishild grab the Goth chief by the arm. Hemnerith turns, shocked and wild-eyed, to punch her away. His elbow finds Eishild's face – the Goth princess flies, backwards, into the sea. Ahes releases herself from his grasp and draws the long knife from the sheath at his belt. She thrusts with both hands – the blade slips on the Goth's armour and cuts his side. In a reflex, Hemnerith swings back. Ahes sways aside to dodge his blade, but she missteps on the slippery stones of the causeway, and the tip of the heavy Gothic sword slashes right across her face.

CHAPTER VI
THE LAY OF MARCUS

It takes a moment before anyone realises what has happened – even Ahes stands in blind, wordless shock. Marcus is the first to cry a howl of anguish. He throws himself into the sea; his men rush after – some to stop him, others to save the Briton princess. I feel a shove from behind: Graelon and Budic finally thrust aside the wagons. Budic and his nobles charge at me and the Iutes, but Graelon stops and stares in stunned silence towards the causeway.

Hemnerith lifts Ahes up and calls at one of his warriors to hand him a wrapping; the water around him turns deep crimson. Blood streams from the deep gash across the girl's eyes and brow, unstoppable, despite Hemnerith's efforts to stem the flow.

Graelon pushes past me, and wades, in what will soon be chest-deep sea, towards his daughter. A chaotic, fierce battle erupts in the middle of the causeway; Marcus and his *equites* on one side, Graelon and his nobles on the other, and in the centre, Hemnerith's Goths, now desperate to break through the Dumnonians to the salvation of the harbour; their heavy armour of mail and scale weighs them down. Hemnerith gives up his effort to save the princess and hands her over to her father, before picking up his sword in both hands and throwing himself into the fray.

I can't do anything to help anyone else as I struggle to lead the men on the island in defence against Budic. I have never been in a fight so muddled and confused; I can't tell who's fighting against whom. The Briton nobles push us

The Song of the Tides

from the beach and into the sea; my boots fill with water. I kill one of Budic's guards and cut another on the shoulder. To my right, Croha fights using both her axes like a sword and shield, parrying with one and striking with the other. To my left, Audulf and Ubba command a group of six Bacauds, trying to break through on Budic's flank and trap him between the wagons. But the Britons are more numerous and more experienced in war than the villagers. Fighting Bacaud rebels is what they've been doing all their lives. The attack falters, and when the Iutes pull back, all but one rebel lies dead in the mud, hued grey with their blood, the petals from the flower carpet dancing on the waves around their bodies.

A dart flies over my head and strikes at the feet of Lord Budic. A javelin pierces the chest of a noble beside him. I turn to see who threw the missiles: it's Hleo, Haering and their little band of Armorican fishermen, come to our rescue.

"Croha, Ubba, Audulf! To boats!" I command. "Eolh, Deor, help me keep the line while they board."

I see no choice but to abandon our Armorican allies to the Briton blades. My duty is to keep my Iutes alive first – then see if I can help Marcus against the Goths. But one glance over my shoulder tells me it's too late to do anything. Hemnerith and Marcus are bound in a fierce, deadly duel, while Graelon stands between them, holding his wounded daughter in his arms, weeping, cursing and kissing her wounds. The sea flows as red as Ahes's dress. Half the Goths are already gone – without a trace, sunk to the bottom in their armour; but so are more than half of the *equites*, their bodies floating on the surface, each in a pool of its own blood.

I board the last of the departing boats, just as the last of the Armoricans falls, pierced by Budic's sword. Eolh and

Deor help push us further into the sea before leaping after us and picking up the oars.

"Get yourselves to the *Maegwind*," I order the others. Warus's ship unfurls its second sail and lifts the anchor, ready to either come to our help, or flee. Its crew won't yet know what happened on the causeway – the island is hiding most of the fighting from their view.

Satisfied that at least my men will be saved from this debacle, I steer my boat back towards the battle. The warriors fight as much against the rolling waves as against each other. Most of them now see to their own salvation from the depths, rather than slaughter. Budic and Father Constantin wade into the sea to drag *Comes* Graelon back to safety – against his protests; two of the nobles pick up his daughter. Ahes, flailing blindly, calls desperately for Marcus; but the *Decurion* is on the other side of the brawl, separated by the entire remaining contingent of the Goths. I spot Drustan help Eishild to reach the safety of dry land. Before long, only Hemnerith, Marcus and a few other warriors remain in the water.

"Ursula!" I cry as we get closer. "Come with us!"

"I'm not leaving Marcus," she replies. She wades up to the *Decurion* and joins his duel against Hemnerith. The Goth warchief fights like a wild boar, despite the wound Ahes cut in his side. The bodies of two *equites* float beside him through the sea of petals, hacked through by his ruby-studded sword. Marcus himself is being pushed back, weary from the struggle against the Goths and the waves. With how deep the water already is, it's clear neither of them hopes to live long enough to get ashore after killing the other. All they care about is each other's death. It's certainly too late for Hemnerith to think of saving himself; the armour would drag him to the bottom like so many of his warriors before he could ever reach the harbour. But Marcus could still be saved – if he still wished to save himself…

I find one last unthrown javelin, rolling on the bottom of the boat. I pick it up and aim; it's a difficult throw in the wobbly vessel, heaving in the waves. As I release it, I already know it will miss. The short, sharp blade only grazes Hemnerith's shoulder. It's enough to distract him. Ursula and Marcus strike from both sides. The *Decurion*'s blade digs into the shield, but Ursula's goes through the block, and her blade goes through the cut in mail on Hemnerith's side, in the same spot where Ahes struck him earlier, only deeper.

I leap into the water. The sea is deep enough to swim; I reach Ursula and help her grab Marcus and pull him away, just as Hemnerith rises back from the deep and lifts his sword like an angry sea demon.

"Leave me," Marcus snarls, and struggles to free himself from our grasp. "Let me kill him."

"You'll die if you stay!"

"I'm dead already."

"She's still alive!" I assure him, but he isn't listening. His eyes are bloodshot and burning with madness. He tears his right arm from Ursula's grip and waves his sword towards Hemnerith, but the two are too far apart already. The Goth wades towards us; waves crash against his chest; the sea spray washes against his face. I can't hold on to Marcus for much longer. I raise my sword and hit him over the head with the pommel. He slumps in my arms.

"Help me get him onto the boat," I urge Ursula. The *Decurion*'s body is heavy and slippery; we almost overturn the vessel with our effort. At last, we all find ourselves on board, heaving, breathless, soaked in seawater, sweat and blood.

"Swiftly – take us to the *Maegwind*," I command the oarsmen. "She won't be waiting for us long."

"And then what?" asks Ursula.

I turn to take one last glance at the bloody scene. A handful of the *equites* crawls back onto the mainland to make one last stand against the surviving Goths, even fewer in number. On the other side of the sunken causeway, Graelon, Budic and the Briton nobles gather over their princess, with Father Constantin applying some sticky ointment to her wounds. And in the middle of it all, rising from the depths like a rock, is warchief Hemnerith, holding his gleaming sword high over his head, the ruthless, blood-red sea pouring into his mouth as he roars his final challenge over the rumble of the waves.

"Then," I reply, turning away from the slaughter, "we're taking him back home."

I breathe a sigh of relief only when we reach the familiar high shore of the harbour at Isca.

All through our journey from Gesocribate, I feared Graelon's pursuit would catch up to us; every time I spotted a sail on the horizon, every time we passed by a harbour on Armorica's northern coast, my heart raced in anxiety. We were too few, too weary, too injured to stand against any

The Song of the Tides

force sent to destroy us by Ahes's vengeful father. But Warus was too skilled a captain, and in command of too fine a ship, to let himself be caught in familiar waters. In the end, the last of the pursuing vessels broke away as soon as we reached the halfway point between Armorica and Britannia. The rest of our journey north was uneventful and, with good winds, mercifully brief.

"Tell Marcus we're home," I say to Croha.

"He will not care," says Ursula as the girl runs off to search for the *Decurion* below deck.

"No, I don't think he will. Would *you*?"

"I would not fall into a drunken stupor," she replies coolly.

"I don't know what I would do if I lost you like this," I say. "Didn't you say this was what you feared the worst? Being separated by Fate, rather than simply through death in battle?"

"It *was* a battle, Octa," she says. "And Ahes knew what she was getting herself into. We all did."

"Why are you so angry about this?" I ask, surprised at the steely note in her voice.

She sighs. "Oh, I don't know… Somehow, it annoys me to see a grown man fall apart like this. He should be proud of Ahes. She fought like a warrior. She was the first to bleed Hemnerith. I would wish you to be proud of me if I did the same."

"You can be sure of that," I say firmly.

She lays her hand on mine. "You will speak to your father?"

"I gave you my word."

Croha, assisted by two of Warus's crewmen, emerges from below deck, hauling Marcus with them. The *Decurion* is as drunk as he's been the past two days, ever since he discovered the ship's stock of heady, dark Burdigalan wine.

"Wha' do you want from me?" he slurs.

"You're home, *Decurion*."

He raises a blurry gaze towards the cliff. "My home is in Armorica, with Ahes," he says. "We're supposed to get wedded, you know."

I give Ursula a worried look. Has the drink addled his mind so much?

She steps up to Marcus – and slaps him across the face. "Lord's wounds, get a hold of yourself! Think how she's suffered for you and your love! Show her some respect and clean yourself up!"

Ursula's outburst sobers the *Decurion* somewhat. He staggers back and looks around, as if for the first time realising where he is.

"My men…"

The Song of the Tides

"Last I saw them, they were breaking out of Gesocribate," I say. "They'll be waiting for your return in hiding, I'm sure. As will Ahes."

"My return?" He scoffs. "I have nothing to return to. Or with. Those were all the men I could spare. The Goths have no doubt already hunted them down."

"What kind of a commander abandons his men in need?" Ursula snarls. "Octa chased after me across half of Gaul. Captain Warus already promised to take you and whatever force you can gather back to Armorica, as soon as you're ready."

"Are you going back with me?"

I shake my head. "Not this time, *Decurion*." I nod at my Iutes. It is a miracle that we didn't lose anyone in the battle at Cair Inis, but they all have gained new scars and wounds fighting Graelon's nobles and helping the Armoricans in their rebellion. "We were supposed to be your wedding guests, not your brothers in arms. Our part is done. Now, we need to heal and rest."

He rubs his eyes, nods and staggers away. One of the crewmen leads him to the water barrel.

I look to the shore. The harbour is empty and silent. Nobody's waiting for us – we arrived unannounced, and earlier than expected; Saint James's Eve, the day when Marcus and Ahes were supposed to be wedded, is today.

"What was it all for?" I wonder aloud.

"What do you mean?" asks Ursula.

"I know what we achieved at Trever and in Wened — but why did we fight on that causeway?"

"We stopped the Goths from taking over Armorica," says Ursula.

"Did we? We only killed a handful. You heard Eishild — the *Rex* of the Goths will not even notice the loss. And we probably did him a favour by slaying his brother. Even if we did push the Goths out of Armorica for now, we have only left it to the likes of Graelon and Budic, to continue their slaughter of the innocents."

"Not every victory is a triumph," she says. "And not every loss a disaster."

"I simply would like to think all those men didn't die in vain."

"Everything is part of the Lord's plan, though we may not see it now."

I smile and hug her close. "Sometimes I wish I had the hopefulness of your faith, Ursula. It must make things so much easier."

She looks at Marcus — her gaze full of worry now, rather than anger. The *Decurion* stands at the railing, staring longingly at the southern horizon. "Faith alone is not always enough," she says. "Maybe we shouldn't be leaving him here alone, after all."

"We brought him home. He's got other friends than us here, I'm sure. Come —" I tug on her shoulder. "— looks like the ship's about to moor. I'm eager to see how our ponies have fared in our absence – they must have missed us greatly."

I find my father by his desk in his small Rutubi house, poring over a letter.

"Father."

He looks up. "Ah, Octa! You're back! They didn't tell me." He glances out the window. "You're early. How was the wedding?"

"There wasn't one."

He raises an eyebrow. "Oh? Did the *Decurion* change his mind, after all?" He chuckles.

"Father, I –"

"Never mind – you'll tell me later. It's good you're here; maybe you'll be able to confirm some of what Hildrik writes about in this letter."

"Bad news?"

"For some. Hildrik tells me the rumours were true – Imperator Maiorianus was killed, and there's unrest in Rome. Aegidius says he will not accept anyone the Romans elect without his approval. The *foederati* tribes are considering tearing up the treaties. Looks like there might be a new war soon." He rolls up the letter and slaps his knee with it. "See – this is exactly what I want our kingdom to avoid. All this squabbling over succession, elections, noblemen, Senators…

The Imperators of old knew it best – a dynasty, even of adopted sons, is just so much more resilient. You haven't heard anything about this in Armorica?" he asks. "Hildrik says Goth riders have been sighted near the River Liger – that's practically on Armorica's border?"

"The Goths… Yes, I think I might have heard a thing or two."

He gives me a sharp look, and only now notices the scar on my brow, where the Goth warchief struck me in the ravine ambush. He stands up, walks up to me and turns my face to the light.

"You have been fighting?" he asks. "Was it pirates?"

"No, Father – it was the Goths."

"The *Goths*! Then Hildrik was right! Is this why the wedding was off?"

"I will explain everything, Father, but first, please – I have something important to tell you."

"Yes, of course. What is it?"

"I intend to get wedded."

He laughs and slaps me on the shoulder. "At last, son!" He stops and gives me a suspicious stare. "It is with Ursula, right? You haven't found some Armorican wench on your journey?"

"No, Father. It is Ursula."

"Good, good. Finally found the courage, eh?" He goes back to his desk and picks up the stylus. "Let me send for her parents. We must begin negotiation at once."

"*Negotiations?*"

"Of course there will be negotiations. Don't worry, I will handle everything. It shouldn't take more than two, three months at most."

"Three months!" I exclaim. "We don't want any ceremony; a simple ritual will suffice…"

He lays down the stylus and looks back to me. "You're the *aetheling* of the Iutes, son," he says, sounding surprised at my protests. "The first there ever was. And you're being wedded into one of the wealthiest and most noble families in Cantiaca. There is nothing simple about it. The future of our tribe may depend on how we arrange your union. Now, why don't you sit down and tell me what happened in Armorica while I write. What were you doing fighting the *Goths*? Can't I send you abroad even once without you getting yourself involved in some other local conflict?"

By the end of the third day of the wedding feast, Ursula, her face flushed with drink and her eyes blurry, finds me by one of the great tents, set up on the flood plain north of Dorowern to accommodate the guests. There are far more people here than there were at Honorius's and Madron's betrothal – but then, my father promised enough meat and ale for everyone who came, and most of the guests are poor serfs and village folk from all over his domain – and beyond.

The colourful tents across the River Stur, with the largest of them flying the banner of three *seaxes*, belong to Aelle and his Saxons. This is the first time he's come to Cantia since the invasion three years ago, taking the opportunity of the truce my father declared for the duration of the wedding to discuss renewing relations and trade between our two peoples. There are Angles and Ikens from the north, Gewisse from the west, Briton merchants from as far away as Callew – and of course, a shipful of Franks, though neither Hildrik nor Basina could come, busy preparing for the approaching conflict in Gaul.

There is one delegation missing in all of this. *Dux* Ambrosius sent no representatives, in what was no doubt a deliberate snub, showing how little he cared for the politics of distant regions and petty kingdoms at the far end of Britannia. Marcus is absent, too, and we heard nothing from him, but we expected that – we did not insist on his presence, knowing how much it might hurt him to see the happiness of others while he was still separated from his beloved. The only Westerner who arrived to Dorowern was Mullo, never one to miss an opportunity for a free drink.

"You're not making merry, *husband*?" Ursula asks playfully.

The ceremony was brief and simple, just as we requested, and took place on the very first day of the celebrations, before even most of the guests arrived at the field of feasting. There were no priests – neither Christian nor Iutish ones; no gods or God were needed to confirm what we already knew. Everything was done according to the Briton custom; I wedded Ursula as my mother's son, not as a Iute, for barbarians, by the Roman law, are still forbidden to marry citizens. We spoke the short vows before my father, Ursula's parents, and ten witnesses, all nobles from Dorowern. After that, our parents exchanged the gifts and sealed documents confirming the results of their negotiations. I took no part in these talks, and I don't know what they entailed, nor do I care. The whole thing seemed absurd to me. Ursula had been right all those years: the wedding itself changed nothing between us, changed nothing within me, all it did was ensure that we would stay together, by law, regardless of what alliances or treaties our parents would need to make in the future.

"I've had enough ale for a year," I reply with a soft chuckle. "Where have you been?"

"I was teaching Deor some *druis* magic," she says.

"*Druis* magic?" I ask, then I remember. "*Oh*."

"He hopes to use it on Croha tonight. Did you know they're lying together?"

"Good for them. Mullo will be inconsolable."

She laughs. "*That* old goat! He could be her father!"

"I doubt he'd ever try anything. He was just admiring her from a distance last time he was here." I step up to her and wrap my arms around her. "You know, you should teach *me* some of that *druis* magic. My father will start asking for an heir one day."

She laughs again, but her smile turns into a grimace. She kisses me and lets me kiss her back; I smell ale and mead on her breath. There's warmth in her embrace and love on her lips, but, as always, little passion in either. I put my hand on her breast; I feel the nipple through the tunic cloth, hardened by the cool autumn breeze, and my manhood rises. As at every Iutish wedding, the darkness around us is filled with moans and groans of couples, believing a wedding night is the most auspicious one to conceive – especially a wedding night of the king's son.

"Please," I say, "let me lie with you."

"You are my husband," she replies. "I must do as you command."

I wince. "Not like that. Show me how to please you. I may not be Donwen, but I'll try my best."

She sighs gently. "Meet me at our tent. I will bathe myself first. I reek of mead."

"I don't mind."

"I'm sure you don't. But just because I wedded a barbarian, doesn't mean I have to make love like one," she says with a grin.

Some stories just refuse to end.

The winter, like all winters, passes quiet and calm. Ursula and I spend most of it settling into our new home: the small *villa* on the road from Rutubi to Dubris, the same one where I used to train my warriors. Once, it belonged to a friend of Ursula's family, before he abandoned it to sail to Armorica or Gallaecia, nobody knew exactly where. According to the treaties signed between our parents, the entire property now belongs to the Iutes, and after settling a few lacking families among the still fertile fields and orchards, we went to work fortifying the grounds around the *Domus* and turning it into a

The Song of the Tides

burh of my own, and a training ground for my bear-shirt guard.

But as soon as the storms abated, bad news came pouring in from across the Narrow Sea. The new Imperator signed peace with the old enemies and gave the Goths and the Burgundians all the territories won from them at such great cost by Maiorianus. The old *Magister Militum* in Gaul, Agrippinus, had been brought back into the Empire's graces and was preparing to march against Aegidius, and his ally, Hildrik.

What was odd about all these rumours and reports was how distant and alien they now sounded to my ears. I knew most of the men involved in these events, some of them I called my friends; and yet, in my quiet, rural abode, it all seemed like a dream. The fertility of our pigs, the coming month of sowing, the new earthen embankment we had to reinforce with wooden planks, or the new irrigation ditches that needed digging, all this occupied my mind far more than the wars and crises on the Continent. It was as if my exploits of the past few years, once turned into a song of a *scop*, turned into a remote myth, a tale from a different era. I could scarcely believe that I was the same Octa who fought at Trever, Wened and Armorica.

One crisp early spring morning, however, seven months almost to the day after we sailed from Gesocribate, the myth comes back to life and returns in the form of two riders, appearing on the road from Dubris.

"I was told I will find the *aetheling* of the Iutes here!" one of them announces in a loud, familiar voice.

"Drustan!"

Ursula and I rush to the gate – a timber construction, not yet finished, marking the western boundary of our little fortress – to welcome the unexpected visitors.

"Is that – Eishild?" Ursula exclaims, seeing the girl riding next to the Drustan. She's wearing the shining mail shirt and red cape of an *eques*.

"Then Marcus came back for you, after all!" I say, helping Eishild off her horse.

"He did, yes." Drustan nods. "Though it took him several long months to find us all."

"How many of you survived?" asks Ursula.

"Seven returned out of twenty," the rider replies grimly.

"And Ahes?" I ask.

"The princess –" He starts, then falls into uncomfortable silence.

"Come, you will tell us all about it," I say, and call for a servant to take the horses to what remain of the *villa's* stables. "You'll have to excuse the state of the place – we only got it a few months ago; everything is still being rebuilt. Our house is small, and –"

"Please, *aetheling*, *Domna* Ursula," the *eques* raises his hand in protest. "I lived in the forests of Armorica for many cold weeks. I will be content with a roof and some furs for bedding."

The Song of the Tides

"I'm sure we can offer more than that," says Ursula. "This way – mind that ditch!"

"I'm glad to see you all here," says Drustan, raising a mug of mead. "There have been too many evenings where I thought I'd never see a friendly face again."

Since all my warriors live on, or near, the grounds of the *villa* now, it was easy to gather everyone who fought with us in Armorica for the evening meal – except Croha, still training to join my father's *Hiréd* under Betula's guidance.

"The Britons hunted us through the woods and marshes," he continues his tale. "Many of Wenelia's men perished to save us from capture. Even their sacrifice wasn't enough – we were cut off on the cliffs of Penhir, on Armorica's westernmost edge, when the *Decurion* finally landed in Gesocribate, some three months after he left it, with what looked like the entire Dumnonian cohort. Lord alone knows how he convinced *Comes* Urbanus to let him take that many warriors across the Narrow Sea."

"That explains why he wouldn't come to our wedding," I note to Ursula.

"I hear he threatened to raze Worgium to the ground when he arrived," Drustan continues. "I've never seen him this wrathful before."

"He came fighting for his love," I say. "There is no greater force to drive a man."

"I wish I had been there to see Marcus reunited with Ahes again," says Ursula.

"Ahes wasn't there anymore when Marcus returned," says Drustan. "The Goths took her with them to Tolosa," he explains, and it's as if the lamp light dimmed around the room.

"I can't believe Graelon just let them take her," says Ursula, the first to speak after a long silence. "Then all we did was in vain, after all."

"I can't imagine the Goths gave him much choice," says Audulf. "Even after the battle on the causeway, there had to be enough left of them to threaten his destruction."

"The Goths are the real reason for our coming here," says Drustan, reaching for a piece of carved piglet's side.

"Then it is as I feared," says Ursula. "You're not here simply to visit old friends."

"That, too, of course, my dear *Domna* Ursula," he says with a smile. "But I bring important news – and a proposition that I hope will interest you and your *Rex*."

"You're talking about the Goths preparing for war with Aegidius," I guess and take a sip of the mead. "We know all about it."

"What you wouldn't know," says Eishild, "is who's going to lead the Goth army in that campaign."

"Is it one of your uncles?" I ask, suspicious as to why it should matter to us.

"Two of them," replies Eishild. "Fridurik – and Hemnerith."

"Hemnerith's alive?" Ursula exclaims and stands upright. "*How?*" she demands, slamming her fist on the table.

"We don't know," says Eishild. "Someone saved him – or he saved himself with some Gothic magic, despite the wounds… However it happened, he lives, and he's commanding troops again. It was he who took Ahes with him – no longer as a bride, but as plunder – a reward for his losses at Inis Cair. Graelon was forced to obey, and to swear his allegiance to my uncles. Any day now, we expect them to launch a diversion from Armorica to assist Theodrik's invasion of Gaul."

I tug gently at Ursula's tunic and nod at her to sit down.

"This is indeed dire news," I say, calmly, sensing what he's about to request. "And if we could help, I wouldn't hesitate… But I don't know what you'd expect from us."

"My *Decurion* requests one last act of friendship," says Drustan. "We're sailing to Gaul to join Aegidius's army – but we alone are too few to make a difference."

"If you're too few, then what good are we?" I ask. "I couldn't spare more than twenty riders, even if I did consider this to be a good use of my recruits. In a war between the Gauls and the Goths, even our combined force will be but a drop in the great ocean."

"We're not going there to fight the Goths," says Eishild. "We're going to find Hemnerith – and this time, we'll make sure he's really dead."

"We ask you to help us free Princess Ahes, and avenge our fallen comrades," adds Drustan. "And Eishild believes she knows how we can do just that."

"Didn't you just say Ahes was in Tolosa? Do you expect us to scale the walls of the Gothic capital?"

"Hemnerith will have the princess in his camp," says Eishild. "He rarely lets her leave his side. My agents assure me of it."

I glance to Ursula, then look at the other warriors gathered around the table. Audulf and Ubba nod reluctantly. Eolh and Deor, hot-blooded youths that they are, tighten their grips on the meat-carving knives as if they were *seaxes*. At last, Ursula nods, too.

"If it's to help Ahes — we have to hear them out, at least," she says. "We have to finish what we started."

"Very well. Let me hear that great plan of yours," I say with a heavy sigh.

The Song of the Tides

CHAPTER VII
THE LAY OF HEMNERITH

The last of the Iutes descends from the ship and stares around, with his mouth gaping and his eyes open wide. For the fifty men who arrived at Rotomag on Aegidius's old *liburna*, this is the first time they have ever seen a Roman town outside Britannia. The first land they see beyond Cantia, where they were born: these are all youths, of the generation raised after Eobbasfleot; none of them remembers the Old Country. And though the town looks little different from the likes of Dubris or Dorowern, and the land beyond its walls still resembles Cantia more than any other place on Earth, the young warriors appear excited as children, as impressed by it all as if we landed in Rome itself.

It takes a while for Audulf to gather them all together, like curious sheep, and march to the camp outside the town's gates, where we join the other fifty warriors who were brought by the same ship from Wecta and Meon four days ago. I find Hildrik waiting for me at the entrance to my tent.

"Is this the last transport?" he asks.

"That's the last of them, yes," I say. "As much of the *fyrd* as my father could spare."

"And I am grateful for it."

"Just remember – we are here as allies of *your* kingdom, not of Gaul or Rome."

The Song of the Tides

The only reason *Rex* Aeric is able to send even this small contingent is the strength of our alliance with the Salians and *Magister* Aegidius. On its way from Wecta, the great *liburna* sailed close past New Port, in the show of force that was to prove to Aelle that Rome is still near, and watchful, and that she knows how to take care of her friends. We can only hope that it was enough to convince the Saxons to refrain from harassing our borders while a *centuria* of our youngest warriors – and twenty of my best riders – is busy fighting the Empire's wars on the Continent.

"Of course," the Salian *Rex* replies with a slight nod. "I'm glad your father and I came to this agreement. I am eager to see your famed bear-shirts in action," he says.

He doesn't even mention the hundred youths, and he's right to dismiss them as mere spear fodder. They were sent here to gain practice and knowledge of fighting a pitched battle and, if they survive at all, a share of glory and plunder that they can take back to their homesteads, but neither Hildrik nor I expect them to be of much use other than filling out the gaps in his flanks.

"We march out soon, then?" I ask.

"Whenever you're ready. I have news from Aegidius. He's on the move already – and expects to meet the Goths on the River Liger."

"I don't know where that is," I remind him.

"Only a few days' ride from Redones, by the stone roads," says Hildrik. "Hemnerith will be eager to reach Armorica's border by Sunday, if his army is to make a difference."

"Then we shall meet him before then. My men will be ready at dawn."

"I'll tell you this much – I'll be glad to live a long life without ever seeing this place again," I say as we descend from the chain of downs that marks the southern border of Belgica province, and ride out onto the vast, sprawling plain, down the old Roman road that leads into Armorica, towards the cathedral city of Redones.

Marcus merely nods. He gazes with a dour, cold stare at the road before us. The last time we rode this highway, he didn't yet know Ahes existed; we searched for Graelon, a mysterious leader of the Briton settlers in Armorica, with little clue as to what we would find. Now, his beloved princess is rotting in Gothic captivity, her father is our enemy, and we march across the province not as a handful of riders on a quest, but as a vanguard of an army. Some distance behind us, still hidden by the downs, are two cohorts of Hildrik's Frankish warriors – and the *centuria* of young Iutes, under Audulf's command.

Our forward patrols confirmed what Hildrik already expected: that Hemnerith's warband had gathered around Redones, together with Graelon's soldiers, ready to pounce on Aegidius's western flank, just as the *Magister Militum* is gathering his Legion to stop the main Gothic army from crossing the frontier on the River Liger.

That is where the war will truly happen. According to Hildrik, Aegidius has gathered the various fortress cohorts and border *centuriae* into one full Legion at his command, nearly five thousand trained men, and filled out his flanks with the Alan and Burgundian *auxilia*. Fridurik, the Gothic commander, is expected to bring at least twice as many with him. Compared to that mighty clash, our mission is merely a diversion; but its importance must not be underestimated. Hemnerith's band is the only Gothic force north of the Liger. If he is allowed to pour across the border into Gaul unchecked, he will be free to ravage the rear of Aegidius's army, with disastrous consequences. If Roman Gaul is to be saved, he must be stopped…

At least, that is one version of what we're doing here. The truth, as always in this twisted, dark age, is more complex. By Roman law, it is Aegidius who is the usurper; the Goths and Graelon's Britons are allies of the Empire, and we are its enemies and traitors – for as long as the current Imperator sits on the throne in Rome. All of this could change before the battle ends; some other Imperator might break the pact with *Rix* Theodrik, or find some other, more reliable ally among the Burgundians or Saxons. It wouldn't be the first time Rome has used one barbarian kingdom against another. There is nothing solid or stable anymore in this world. Politics, diplomacy, warfare, alliances and enmities, all of it shifts like the winds and currents of the sea, and adrift in this storm is the rudderless ship of Rome herself.

Not that any of this matters to the Iutes or the Franks. Hildrik marches to war to stop the Goths from becoming too powerful; he doesn't care for Aegidius or Rome – but he needs the Roman province separating him from the Gothic kingdom to stay strong, at least as long as the Franks themselves are not strong enough to stand against their enemies on their own. My father agrees with him; he couldn't care less about Aegidius, but he fears Theodrik's victory more – or rather, the power void that would result in the Roman defeat.

Myself and Marcus are here as neither an ally of Aegidius nor of Hildrik. No matter what the Frankish king and the *Magister* might believe, our only goal is to find Ahes – and kill Hemnerith, if we can.

"I think we're close enough," says Eishild when we reach ruins of a *mansio* on an old crossroad. "We should set up camp here. Any closer and Hemnerith will grow suspicious."

"I agree," I say. "Ubba, ride back to Hildrik; tell him to stay in the foothills. Ursula, come with me – we'll go look for Wenelia. She should be somewhere in the woods near Redones." I turn back to Eishild. "I do hope this plan of yours will work, *Fraujo*."

"Believe me, *aetheling*," she says, "nobody prays more for our success than me."

My heart is pounding, and my brow is covered with sweat. I'm telling myself it's anxiety about the success of the plan, rather than fear for my own life. I have seen what the Goths do with their prisoners, and I have no way of knowing if they respect the flag of truce, though Eishild assures me that not even Hemnerith will dare to violate our banner, painted with the *chrismon* and the word *Pax* written in Gothic letters, as she advised.

The guards stop me on the approach to the Gothic camp. I notice that Graelon and the Britons set up their own tents at some distance, across a narrow stream, clearly not trusting their new allies enough to share a camp with them. I command the guards to announce my arrival to their warchief.

The Song of the Tides

"Tell him the man who defeated him at Cair Inis is here to talk."

I wait a long time for their return, all the while exchanging silent stares with the remaining Goths. I doubt they know what I'm talking about. There must be over a thousand warriors here; only a few would've accompanied Hemnerith to Armorica the first time, and I don't think the warchief would've allowed the tale of his defeat to spread throughout the warband.

When Hemnerith finally appears, the reason for my wait becomes clear. He doesn't walk up to me – he is brought to meet me on a litter carried by four Hispanic slaves. He gives me a suspicious look, and it's clear he doesn't recognise me.

"I thought you were Marcus," he says gruffly. "If you were, I would've cut you down on the spot, flag or no flag." He's lying on one side; the other, where Ahes and Ursula struck him, is bulging with soft padding. That he would rather suffer the indignity of this transport than invite me to his tent for the talks tells me he's as afraid of some treachery on my part as I am of his. "Who in *halja* are you?"

"Octa, *aetheling* of the Iutes," I introduce myself. "We fought at Marcus's side on the causeway. It was my wife who gave you this wound," I add, pointing to the padding.

His eyes narrow. "And is the wench with you, too?"

"She is." I nod. "As is *Decurion* Marcus."

"You must be marching with the Franks. What do you want? Has Hildrik sent you to plead?"

"He sent me to bargain."

He scoffs. "That upstart has nothing worth bargaining for. I will crush his puny band tomorrow and march on to meet my brothers at Aurelianum. What could you possibly offer to make me reconsider?"

"How about your dead brother's daughter?"

His cheeks turn crimson. He lifts himself up on his elbow and winces. "Eishild? That treacherous heretic's alive?" he booms. "What would I need her for?"

After the battle at the causeway, the Goths searched for Eishild, who fled with Drustan and the surviving *equites* into Armorica's forests; but they soon gave up the hunt. Eishild believed her uncles must have been glad to see her disappear. At least that way, nobody could have blamed them for my death. Besides, they were soon too busy with the coming war to worry about some lost noble girl.

"I know there are many among your warriors who would not be so keen to heed your orders if they knew you let Thaurismod's daughter perish in heathen thraldom," I reply, struggling to keep calm as the spears of Hemnerith's guards reach a little too close to my flesh for comfort.

The warchief calms down, though his face is still red and his eyes still narrowed in anger. "How do I even know you're telling the truth?" he asks.

"You can see her for yourself. Come to the *mansio* on the crossroad tonight. She will be there – as will Hildrik, to discuss the terms of your withdrawal."

The Song of the Tides

The Goth laughs so hard, he almost falls off the litter. The Hispanic slaves struggle to keep him upright. "*Withdrawal?* You overestimate how much that girl is worth to me. But —" He stops and scratches his arse. "I do want to see if my dear niece is unharmed. I will send one of my men to check on her."

"Not your men. Yourself."

"Do you take me for a fool? You think I would just walk into whatever trap you set for me in that village?"

"I didn't say you should come alone. You can come with your guard. And your spies will tell you, no doubt, of the size of our vanguard. You know very well it's impossible to set up an ambush in these empty plains."

He twirls the end of his moustache, then claps at the slaves. They turn around.

"I'll be there," he shouts as they carry him away. "And you better pray I don't find a single scar on Eishild's pretty little face. Maybe I can still use her as a bride after all this. That's all she's ever been good for."

"They're coming," Eolh reports, returning from his hideout. "And it's just as you predicted."

"How many are there?" asks Ursula.

"Twenty riders in front. The rest are behind them, trying to be stealthy."

[146]

I leap up. "Bring Eishild," I tell Ursula. "Prepare yourselves. Are the ponies ready?"

"Ready as they'll ever be, *aetheling*," replies Hleo, standing to attention.

"Good. Remember, I don't want anyone to get hurt needlessly."

In the middle of the dusty crossroad, by the moss-grown milestone, we establish the meeting point: a couple of iron folding stools, a barrel of ale, and the white horse banner on a spear shaft. Behind it, my warriors spread a barrier of logs and thorns across the road. Only a handful of my Iutes are left in the *mansio*; the rest I sent away with Marcus's *equites* back to Hildrik's camp, not wishing to startle Hemnerith into retreating too soon.

Ursula returns from the ruined building, with Eishild in tow. With her tussled hair, cheeks smudged with ash and grime, torn and dishevelled tunic, she looks just like someone who's spent a long time in barbarian captivity. She arrives just in time, too; just as I sit her down and tie her to the stool, Hemnerith's warriors ride into the *mansio* grounds. The Gothic noblemen were already an imposing presence back at Cair Inis, with their heavy armour and immaculate, long golden hair adorning their heads like diadems. Here, they are even more striking, coming astride great warhorses, each of the warriors wielding a heavy two-handed lance and a large painted shield.

"If they charge at us, they will crush us into dust," Ursula remarks quietly.

I nod at Marcus. He steps behind Eishild and draws his sword. I approach the nearest of the riders with my hands held before me to show I'm unarmed.

"Where's Hemnerith?" I ask.

The rider laughs and lowers his lance until its point touches my chest.

"Did you really think my *Frauja* would come at your bidding, heathen?"

He takes a look around, at Eishild, Marcus and the thin line of Iutes cowering behind the barricade with their spears and shields.

"Where's Hildrik?" he asks in return.

"I'm supposed to send for him if all goes well."

He smacks his lips and murmurs something to himself in his language. The other Goths snigger.

"Your master promised," I say, holding the shaft of his lance.

"We don't need to keep oaths made to the *wildeis*," the rider scoffs. He tears the lance out of my grip, then turns to his men. "Get them."

"Run!" I manage to cry before the rider grabs me, lifts me up with one hand and throws me over his saddle. Another charges up to Ursula, hits her over the head with the butt of his lance and picks her unconscious body from the ground. Marcus drops his sword in pretend fear and leaps back, scrambling over the blockade while my Iutes abandon the defences and run to their mounts. The riders stop to drag Marcus from the logs and release Eishild from her binds, but by the time they get around the barricade, my men are already safely away, hidden from sight by a cloud of dust raised by the hooves of their ponies. The Goth commander barks an impatient order. The riders halt their pursuit and turn obediently back.

"I can't believe *Frauja* Hemnerith got bested by the likes of you," the Goth chuckles. "He must have been drunk with love! If all of Hildrik's men are as foolish and cowardly as yours, tomorrow we'll have not a battle, but a slaughter!"

He laughs again and, as I try to lift myself to sit in the saddle, he punches me into darkness.

At nightfall, the screaming stops.

In the darkness of the stuffy tent, I reach out as far as I can with my tied hands to reach Ursula. Our fingers touch; she moves closer, and now we can clasp our hands.

"He knew what they would do to him," she whispers. "Still, he agreed to the plan."

They took Marcus away first, and we haven't seen him since – but we've heard him all through the day. I doubt if Hemnerith wants to draw some confession about Hildrik's battle plans out of him – it's far more likely he ordered the *Decurion* tortured simply out of spite, as revenge for the humiliation at the causeway.

The Song of the Tides

"What if they're going to kill him?" I ask.

"They'd lose a valuable hostage," Ursula replies without conviction. "They could've killed him at the crossroads…"

My question is answered a moment later when someone throws Marcus into the tent. The *Decurion* groans in pain.

"I'll deal with you two tomorrow," says the torturer, before leaving all three of us in the darkness.

There's nothing left for us to do but wait as the camp around us quietens for the night. I shift my body to make myself more comfortable, but it's difficult with both my hands and legs tied tight. I don't know when I fall into an uneasy, fragile sleep, interrupted from time to time by the hooting of owls, and shouts of the guards calling to each other across the camp. It must be well past midnight when I'm wakened by someone entering the tent in silence.

I hear the ring of a knife drawn from a leather sheath, and feel it cut through the binds at my hands. Our rescuer then moves to Ursula and, after cutting her ropes, comes back to me and puts the knife in my hand.

"Blessed be the Lord Jesus Christ, the only-begotten Son of God," the man whispers quickly in my ear before leaving the tent.

With a groan, I scramble to my hands and feet. I rub my eyes and strain my gaze, but all I can see in the darkness is a sliver of moonlight peering through the tent flap.

"Are you alright?" I ask Ursula.

"I'm fine," she replies. "They were gentler with me."

"What was that he whispered to us?"

"The Roman Creed," Ursula says. "To show he's with Eishild."

I shake my head. "I will never understand this Christian preoccupation with minute details of your faith."

"It doesn't matter. What matters, for now, is that Eishild was right – we *do* have allies in this camp, however few they may be."

I move over to Marcus and stir him gently awake.

"Can you walk?" I ask.

He sits up with a moan. "I… think so." He rubs his temple. "But I won't be much good in a fight."

"That's alright," says Ursula. "As long as we don't have to carry you. You've bought us time with your sacrifice. We can't ask you for any more."

"Good, because I don't think I have anything more to give." He tries a chuckle, but it turns into a cough – which draws the attention of the guard outside.

"Hey!" He peers inside. "Quiet down there, or I'll call Badwila to start on you earlier."

"I could kill him right now," I whisper, tightening my grip on the knife.

"Wait." Ursula holds my hand. "Remember the plan."

"Do you really think they'll –?"

Just then, the night erupts with shouts, howls, clash of arms. A few moments later, I hear the guard outside our tent run off in the direction of the noise. Ursula helps Marcus off the ground, and together we sneak carefully outside. Light feet tap behind us: I turn around to see Eishild, carrying a torch and a heavy Gothic sword. She hands the weapon to Ursula.

"His tent is in the eastern part of the camp," she says, "by the stream. Topped with a golden raven."

"Is Ahes there?"

"Yes, but she's –" She glances to where the sound of the fiercest fighting comes from. "You'll see for yourself. Hurry. They will not last long."

The brave warriors striking at the border of the Gothic camp belong to what remains of Wenelia's short-lived uprising. There can't be more than a few dozen of them left; assaulting a thousand Gothic warriors is a suicide mission, even if their night attack came as a complete surprise. Hemnerith could never have expected the Armoricans to be anything more than a completely spent force – and certainly not for them to strike here, on the eastern frontier, far away from the safety of their woods and marshes.

Avoiding the warriors rushing to and fro between the tents and weapon racks, we reach the great white tent, topped with the golden statue of a raven spreading its wings. Two spearmen guard the entrance, flanked by twin burning braziers. We hide in the shadows and watch Hemnerith emerge from inside, supporting himself on an oaken staff.

"*Wardja! Wardja!*" he stops a passing officer and, judging by the tone of his voice and waving of hands, demands from him an explanation of the sudden commotion. He then shouts a few more orders and, satisfied that the situation is under control, turns back to his tent.

"Now," I say and push Eishild out into the light. She runs to Hemnerith, calling his name in a panicked voice. The warchief turns around with an impatient scowl.

"*Hwa –?*" he asks before she throws herself into his arms with a fearful cry. He holds her, awkwardly, unsure what she wants from him. She explains something hurriedly, swallowing tears and gasps. Annoyed, Hemnerith looks around – and, seeing no other warriors to heed his command since everyone else is busy fending off the Bacaud assault, grunts at the two spearmen to accompany the girl back to her tent.

As soon as they leave, Ursula and I sneak after the warchief. I hear him grunting and heaving inside; each move must be causing him a great deal of pain, and I see Ursula's eyes gleam with satisfaction – she knows it was her blade that caused this pain.

We storm inside. Hemnerith stares straight at us. In the corner behind him, I spot Ahes, swaddled in blankets, her left eye under a blindfold. She sits up when we enter, her movements oddly heavy and sluggish. I only have time to notice, with wonder, that her bedding and Hemnerith's are on the opposite sides of the tent, before the Goth chieftain snarls at us and charges at us, wielding his staff like a spear.

The Song of the Tides

I leap forward, dodge the staff and stab him with my knife in the stomach. The blade snaps on the mail coat he wears under the robe. His staff hits my shoulder. I hear a nasty snap, groan and drop to my knees.

"Octa! Ursula!" Ahes calls. She reaches for a bronze lamp stand beside her bedding. "How did you –?"

"Stay back!" Ursula warns her. She jumps over me, whirls the sword and strikes at the warchief's chest – but he parries effortlessly with the staff. He fights well, but without the staff's support, his stance falters. I kick at his legs. He wobbles and steps back. Ursula cuts again, this time evading his defences, and hits his right shoulder. He roars in pain and anger and punches Ursula in the face, throwing her to the ground.

With a loud clang and a sickening crack, the lamp stand in Ahes's hands lands on Hemnerith's skull. Roaring like a wounded boar, the chieftain sways, swirls and strikes her in the head with the staff. She falls down, stunned by the blow. I grab the sword from Ursula's hands and, when he turns back to face me, thrust it straight in Hemnerith's heart. The heavy Gothic blade cuts through mail and bone as if it was straw. Blood bursts from Hemnerith's chest. He collapses with a howl of agony, like a felled tree, flailing his hands.

I pick the still unconscious Ahes up and finally realise why her movements were so slow: she's heavily with child. I have no time to ponder this shocking revelation; I hand her to Ursula, before kneeling over Hemnerith to make sure he's dead. With a dying spasm, he tightens his left hand around a golden *bulla* hanging from his neck. When I stoop to see what it is, his right hand shoots up and grasps my throat. I stab at it repeatedly with the broken shard of my knife until, at last, he lets go. The blood-covered hand falls to the floor.

"Is he – is he dead?" I croak, gasping for air.

Ursula lifts the sword one more time and thrusts it into Hemnerith's neck.

"He is now."

I reach for the *bulla* and pry it from the warchief's dead hand.

"Leave it," Ursula urges. "We have to run."

"Wait – I need to see what was so important…"

I struggle with the mechanism for a moment. It opens only when I lift it with the broken knife blade. Inside is a lock of dark auburn hair.

"It's – Ahes's," says Marcus, looking over my shoulder. He stares astonished at the lock. I notice he's holding a bloodied sword in one hand – and helps Ursula hold Ahes with the other.

"Where did you get that sword?"

"I killed one of the guards," he explains. "The others are already coming back. We have to go." He takes one last glance at the *bulla*, then at Ahes's prominent belly. "What's going on?"

"We'll have plenty of time to wonder back in Hildrik's camp," says Ursula. She picks up Hemnerith's staff and hands me the sword, red with the warchief's fresh blood. "It's going to be a long way back, carrying your woman in this darkness."

"Marcus, you will *have* to go and talk to her," I insist.

The *Decurion* broods over the flickering lamp while Cado, the surgeon, looks to his injuries. The wounds are numerous and painful, but shallow – the Gothic torturer plainly wished for the ordeal to last for a long time, and he knew his job.

"What does it all mean, Octa?" he says quietly. "Why did he have her hair in a locket? Whose child is she bearing?"

"Maybe you should ask her yourself."

"Maybe I don't want to hear the answer."

He clenches his fist over the lamp's flame and holds it until his skin turns bright red. He pulls back with a hiss.

"I have plenty of work already, Marcus," Cado grunts. "I don't need you adding any more injuries."

He steps back, observes his handiwork and nods, approvingly. "I'm done here," he tells me. "You can do with him whatever you want. I'll go see to the princess now."

"Come with us, Marcus," I insist. "For my sake. You dragged us here with you because of Ahes. You owe this to me and Ursula. Give her a chance to explain herself."

Reluctantly, he stands up.

"I shouldn't be surprised," he says as we step out of the tent. "She spent longer in Hemnerith's company than she ever did with me."

"She was forced to, Marcus."

"At first, yes… But who knows what happened after the first few months…"

We follow Cado to Ursula's tent, where Ahes is resting. She no longer wears the blindfold, proudly showing her horrific wound to the world. The scar from Hemnerith's blade runs through her left eye and the top of her nose, but despite the injury, she remains the same auburn-haired beauty Marcus fell in love with all those years ago.

As we enter, she turns her one seeing eye towards us.

"Does it hurt?" I ask her.

"Not anymore," she says. "There were Roman physicians in Tolosa – they have ways to help wounds heal that we forgot in Britannia."

"I'm glad to hear it. It must have been terrible."

She scoffs sadly. "It wasn't the wound that hurt me the most," she says. "I was lost, alone in the darkness – taken from all I knew and everyone I loved. How cruel can the fates be?" She shakes her head. "All I ever wanted was to see the world. And now I can't even see Armorica properly. For a long time I wished Hemnerith had killed me, rather than just mutilate me like this."

"Is that all he did?" Marcus asks.

The Song of the Tides

"My love?" Ahes turns to him. "Whatever do you mean?"

"He took you for a bride," Marcus says, gazing at her belly. "He had the right to bed you, even if you resisted."

"Marcus… He never laid a hand on me," she replies in a pained voice. Though her mutilated face can no longer show her emotions as keenly as before, I can tell Marcus's question wounded her more than Hemnerith's blade. "Nor let anyone harm me. You saw us – we even slept in separate beddings. It's strange, but I do believe, in his own way, he truly loved me… And felt guilty for what he did to me."

The *Decurion* stares at her in stunned silence.

"Then who's –?"

"There is only one man I ever loved," she replies. "And only one man I ever laid with."

"Then – then why was your hair in his *bulla*?"

"Marcus!" Ursula protests. "Did you not hear what she just said? She carries your child!"

"Hemnerith asked me for it," Ahes replies. "How could I refuse such a simple request?"

"What else did he ask of you?" Marcus insists. "What else did you agree to?"

"Nothing!" Ahes replies angrily. She clutches Ursula's hand in hers – her palm trembles with emotion. "Why can't you believe –?"

"I don't know *what* to believe," Marcus says. He stands up. "I have to prepare my men. We ride at dawn," he says and storms off towards his tent.

"If I knew he'd turn out such a fool, I'd never have agreed to follow him here," says Ursula. "He's just covering his own blame for abandoning you." She puts her hand on Ahes's shoulder. "It will be alright. You're back among friends now."

"He's just distraught," I say. "With what happened to you, with the coming battle… I'm sure he'll see sense tomorrow, after it's all done."

"If all goes well," says Ursula.

"I'm certain it will," says Ahes. "Fate owes me a favour."

That Gothic rider was right. This was not a battle – this was a slaughter. With their warchief dead, the Goths, still recovering from the chaos of the night assault, stood little chance against Hildrik's adept command and the prowess of his warriors.

I took no part in the dawn attack, leaving the command of my Iutes to Audulf and Ursula. I couldn't feel it at first, but Hemnerith's staff shattered a bone in my shoulder, so all I could do was observe the battle from a nearby hill. The lightning speed and skill with which the Franks descended upon their enemies was a terrific sight to behold; it almost made our night effort seem pointless. The Gothic heavy cavalry was still forming into a wedge when Hildrik's skirmishers struck their flanks with *francisca* axes and *angon* javelins, thrown with unerring accuracy, punching a great hole in their line, through which shieldsmen and *seax*-men poured like an armoured fist. The battlefield was a muddy flood plain of the same winding stream that separated the Gothic and the Briton camps. Whoever commanded the Goth force after Hemnerith's death, chose it poorly – or was forced to by Hildrik's skilled manoeuvring. The heavy horses got stuck in the mire, too slow to turn against the enemy thrusting against their rear. On the far side of the field, the lightly armed levies and the Iute youths did a good job of distracting the Goth reserves and preventing the spearmen from coming to the riders' aid, though when they were at last forced back, they left many dead in the trampled, blood-grey mud.

Their sacrifice was not in vain. Disheartened by the loss of their commander, and shocked at the suddenness of their defeat, the surviving Goths chose to flee rather than make a stand. Only a handful of riders managed to get back across the stream, where they met their deaths at the swords of Hildrik's cavalry, riding from their dawn charge on Graelon's troops. The sun barely touches the high noon when the first Frankish warriors return to the camp, laden with plunder and captives, filled with the elation of an easy triumph. Not long after, Marcus – having shrugged off the injuries of the night before with remarkable effort – arrives from the Briton camp with a tied-up man in rich, torn robes cast over his saddle.

He throws him to the ground before Ahes. It takes me a moment to recognise his face, battered and bloodied, his left eye swollen and bulging. He rises to his knees and raises his hands in supplication.

"My daughter! Lord bless us – I'm so happy to see you!"

Ahes steps up to her father and stares down at him with her one eye. Graelon looks at her face and starts to weep. Marcus puts his sword to Graelon's neck.

"What do you want me to do with him?" he asks.

"Let him be. Knowing what he allowed to happen to me will be punishment enough," she says.

Graelon prostrates himself in the mud in craven gratitude. Ahes nods at me, and I help her step over her father and approach the *Decurion*. She reaches out and gently touches first his chest, then his face.

"It's over," she says. "You've had your revenge. You can soften your heart now."

He strokes her hands, then falls to his knee and presses his head to her bulging belly. She puts her arms around him. He closes his eyes and listens, in heavy silence. The passion I saw in them before the battle at Cair Inis is gone – but I sense in that first, sombre embrace the slow return of their love.

I glance past them, to see a small crowd of warriors marching in our direction, escorted by a few of my Iute riders. "Who are they?" I ask.

"After we routed Graelon's nobles, the rest of them surrendered and declared they wanted to join us – join their princess," Marcus replies as he releases Ahes from his embrace and takes a step back – still holding her hands, I notice. "They have no love for the Goths. Or so they all claim now that their allies have been vanquished."

The Song of the Tides

In a cloud of dust, Hildrik rides up to us with a triumphant grin. His mood is as different from Marcus's as a bright summer day is from a cold winter's night.

"*Hwet!* We have won a great victory!" he announces, shaking his sword over his head, in case anyone around was in any doubt as to the battle's outcome.

"It appears you didn't need our help after all," I say. "You would've crushed the Goths just as easily with Hemnerith leading them."

"Nonsense!" He leaps from his horse and slaps me on the shoulder – I wince; he hit me right in the broken bone. "I know how these Goths fight. They're fierce enemies when they're serving under a good commander, and Hemnerith was no fool. Now, I'm not saying we *wouldn't* have beaten them, either way," he boasts, "but it would never have been this easy – and we wouldn't have taken so many captives." He points to the long column of men slowly plodding up the hill. "I owe you again, Octa."

"I barely did anything," I say. "It was all – hey!"

I spot Eishild in the front of the column of Goth prisoners, and rush to her, just in time to stop a Frankish warrior's club from falling on her back.

"What do you think you're doing?" I shout, grabbing the Frank's hand.

"Just making sure the wench doesn't slow us down," he snarls.

"This is the niece of the king of the Goths! And you will treat her with the respect she deserves!"

Eishild smiles. "It's alright, Octa," she says. "I'm just a captive like all the others."

I drag her out of the line, ignoring the guard's protests. "But you've helped us so much," I whisper. "You shouldn't even be here with these…"

"Hush." She puts a finger to her lips. "I will stay with my people. I need this pretence if I'm ever to return home. And trust me, I can do more to help my fellow faithful if I'm with them than in whatever foreign land my uncles would exile me to, if I returned to Tolosa."

"I understand – it's just…"

"I'll be fine. I can handle a few blows. Marcus and Drustan won't let me come to any real harm. Now take me back, before those guards start wondering why you're being so friendly with me…"

"I was hoping you would ride with us to Aurelianum," says Hildrik. He tightens the saddle straps and slides his lance into the holster. "I could use those bear-shirts of yours again."

"Ours is a poor and small kingdom; we can ill afford to have a hundred warriors away from home for long," I say. "The truce with the Saxons will not last forever – and the youths are needed home for lambing season."

He nods. "You're right. You've done more than enough."

"Besides," I add, "you have Marcus and his riders to replace us."

The Dumnonians briefly considered returning home as well – like us, they came to Gaul only to help their *Decurion* rescue his beloved; but in the end, Marcus decided to honour his alliance with Rome to the end. "In truth, I don't think I'm ever coming home," he told me when we made ready to part our ways. "Graelon's people say they want Ahes to rule over them in his stead – and she will need me by her side."

"Then you will stay with her?"

"Of course," he scoffed. "I came all this way to win her back – did you think I would leave her just because she may have shared a bed with some Gothic chieftain?"

"You still don't believe the child is yours?"

He paused, and his eyes turned dark and melancholy. "It matters not," he said. "Our love will grow strong again. I am sure of it. No pain lasts forever."

Hildrik lays his hands on my arms – gently, this time; my shoulder is bound in tight wrappings but is still sore and swollen. "I hope we can meet for longer next time, *aetheling*. And I hope my wife will be with us, too. One day I will stop putting children in her belly, I promise!" He erupts in a bawdy laugh.

"You're moving out already?" asks Ursula, appearing behind me with a roasted leg of rabbit in her hand. "It hasn't even been a day. We've barely finished burying our dead."

We lost thirteen men in the battle – all of them the young recruits. Many more got injured, but those who survived were filled with pride of the victory they took part in – though I doubt many of them did anything more than wave a spear and shout as they watched the Franks slaughter the Goths by the dozens.

"Aegidius will need me at his side in a few days," says Hildrik. "Thanks to you, my losses are slight, and we don't need to rest and heal as long as I expected. I don't want to waste this opportunity."

"I can't wait to hear the song of this battle," Ursula says, taking a bite of the rabbit.

"It will be glorious, whatever the outcome," Hildrik replies. He pats his horse's flank. "There are few finer foes left in Gaul than Theodrik's Goths."

"Whatever the outcome?" I ask. "Then you're not certain of victory?"

He shrugs. "Who can ever be certain of anything in this world?" he says philosophically. "We are warriors. Our life is in the hands of the gods. At any moment, it can be cut short by a stray javelin or a sharp spear blade…" The solemn mood doesn't last long, and his expression turns into a broad grin. "But until then, we fight. The Goths have not yet fully recovered after the beating they suffered at Maiorianus's hand. There's a reason why their king is sending his brother to lead the army, rather than himself. No, I'm sure Aegidius will prevail. This time, at least."

He leaps onto the saddle and smacks his lips. The mare neighs and lifts her head, waiting for her master's command.

"Look out for a messenger from Tornac," the king of the Franks says, giving us a Legionnaire's salute. "I'll be sending one as soon as we win."

"We will await the news eagerly," I say, returning the salute. "And when you're done here, come to Cantia, with your queen. We will go for a hunt in Andreda. We may not have bears in our woods – but our wild boars are just as fat and vicious as those in the Charcoal Forest!"

"I can't wait," he says and spurs the horse to a trot. At his signal, the heralds blow the war horns and raise his banner, embroidered with the golden Salian bees – and the entire Frankish army heaves forward behind him like a giant snake.

"Let us hurry home," I say to Ursula, pulling her close. "Even victory tastes bitter in this forsaken country."

James Calbraith

HISTORICAL NOTE

Most of the details of the Breton legend of the Sunken City of Ys, including the extended family of King Gradlon and his wife, Queen Malgven, have been introduced by late-nineteenth-century authors such as Edward Schuré. I chose to base my retelling partly on those details, rather than just the rather austere medieval legend itself.

King Theodoric I of the Goths had indeed many sons, of whom the eldest three were successive leaders of the Tolosan kingdom. The fourth son, Frederic, is mentioned fighting in the Battle of Orleans in 463 AD – forming the background to this novella – but of the remaining two, including Hemnerith, nothing else is known but their names.

The "old faith" of the Goths mentioned here is Arianism – an obscure early version of Christianity which hadn't been regarded as heresy until the full formulation of the Nicene Creed in 381 AD. By then, the Goths, as well as many other Germanic tribes in the East, had already converted from paganism, through efforts of Bishop Wulfila, resulting in a schism which would last for several centuries, with grave consequences to everyone involved.

Printed in Great Britain
by Amazon